The Road to Roma

The Road to Roma
and Other Stories

by

Dave Kuhne

INK
BRUSH
PRESS

ISBN 978-0-9835968-1-3
Library of Congress Control Number: 2011931823

Ink Brush Press
Temple, Texas

Acknowledgments

I am grateful to the editors of the following journals for publishing stories gathered into this collection:

Aries, "Learning the Colors"
Concho River Review, "No Scars Whatsoever"
descant 2000, "The Cook's Tale"
Literary Fort Worth, "Magic Coins"
New Texas 91, "The Bridge at Mountainberg"
New Texas 2000, "The Road to Roma"
Texas Soundtrack, "Ridin' My Thumb to Mexico"

For LR

Other Fiction from Ink Brush Press

Laurie Champion, editor, *Texas Told'em: Gambling Stories,* with an introduction by Doyle Brunson

Terry Dalrymple, *Fishing for Trouble*

Andrew Geyer, *Siren Songs from the Heart of Austin*

Andrew Geyer, *Dixie Fish*

H. Palmar Hall, *Into the Thicket*

Myra McLarey, *The Last Will and Testament of Rosetta Sugars Tramble*

Jim Sanderson, *Faded Love*

Jim Sanderson, *Dolph's Team*

Jan Seale, *Dearness Happens*

Melvin Sterne, *Zara*

CONTENTS

Magic Coins

The magic man appeared when Jake was busy cleaning up the lot—picking up the broken beer bottles and the soiled diapers—sorting through the urban refuse of another one-hundred-and-five degree day in Fort Worth, Texas. The man was Hispanic—Jake still called them Mexicans—and muscular but not too tall. He wore baggy pants that sagged low on his butt, and he had shed his shirt because of the heat. His upper body was covered with tattoos: gang markings (Sur XIII), women's names (Maria, Marta), and odd, pre-Columbian designs that resembled abstract art. The tattoos seemed to move and swarm beneath the sweat that glazed his chest.

"Hey," he demanded, "you work here?"

No, Jake thought, I'm sweeping used diapers off of this stinking lot for fun. But he put on his best retarded-geezer smile and said, "Yeap, how can I help yee?"

"My coin, man. I lost my magic coin. I want it back."

He pointed to one of the wash bays, and Jake realized that the man had deposited his "magic coin" into the slot that dropped quarters into a bay safe.

"What kind of coin is it?"

"Like a quarter, man, but gold. There's a picture of a naked girl on it. Titty side reads 'Heads I Win.' Ass side reads 'Tails You Lose.' It was a couple of weeks ago I lost it here."

Jake knew then that he would probably never find the

coin. Either it was buried beneath all the quarters he needed to count or it had slipped through the counting machine and was in a thousand-dollar bag that, by now, would be sitting in the Federal Reserve Bank in Dallas.

"It's important I get my coin back." The tattooed man shifted his eyes to a car parked in one of the drying bays.

The car was a primer-blotched Chevy Impala with four gangsters hanging onto the doors. The gang members glared at Jake.

"I'm only the clean-up guy. But I can ask the owner if he found any coin like yours. Can you leave a number?"

Jake got a pen and one of the refund forms he left in the mailbox for those who lost money in the machines. The magic man wrote out his name, Cruz, and his number, a 924 exchange that told Jake that he lived somewhere nearby, probably in one of the dilapidated rent houses west of the Baptist Seminary.

"The coin, man. It stands for our honor. We never lose."

"I get it," Jake chuckled. "Heads I win, and tails you lose."

Cruz gave Jake the evil eye before walking away to join his amigos.

Jake knew what sort of coin the man was talking about. Every six months or so he would find one mixed in with the quarters. The coin was a token, the kind that guys fed to the machines at the video-sex shops. Usually, Jake tossed these porno coins into the pits with the other slugs people used to cheat the equipment. But he hadn't seen any porno coins for a long time because—in a raid that was the subject of an on-going lawsuit—Tarrant County's sheriff had shut down most of the X-rated video parlors.

The magic man wasn't the first to lose something at the wash, and if it were possible, Jake was glad to retrieve lost keepsakes. At least once a week someone lost, or thought he lost, a precious ring in one of the vacs. Then Jake would have to unlock the vac trap and shovel through the accumulated dust and filth in search of a lost treasure that, more often than not, would never be found. One time a guy dropped his false teeth into one of the bay pits, and Jake helped him fish them out. Jake warned the man that people had been known to relieve themselves in the pits. And there was the time a fellow from the Philippines accidentally deposited a New York subway token in the coin slot. The man begged Jake to look for it, saying it was his good luck charm, the first thing he got when he came to America. Jake emptied the safe and found the man's token. But that had been easy. The subway token was only in the vault a few minutes when the man asked for it back. It was unlikely that Jake could find a coin deposited weeks ago.

"Magic coin my ass," Jake mumbled to himself as the gangsters drove away.

Jake never put much credence in magic; he was a logical, reasonable American who got up every morning, went to work, and put his faith in electricity, physics, and mechanics —all the things that kept the machines at his car wash moving, pumping, turning, working. Magic was okay for others, he thought, but not for him. As much as he might like to, he couldn't wave a juju, grigri, fetish, amulet, or talisman over a broken pump and expect it to repair itself. He couldn't blow some cigarette smoke out his nose, recite an incantation, wave his arms around and expect a broken hose to seal its wound. No, machines did not work that way, and neither did the world, at least not the world according to Jake.

Jake had owned the wash ever since his father died and Jake quit his job teaching industrial arts at Paschal, one of the city's largest high schools. Jake was tired of dealing with high school kids—many of them were gangsters or wannabe gangsters and some of them were mean as panthers—and he found that his mechanical skills came in handy at the wash; there was always something that needed repair. He was good at mechanics and welding when he started working the lot, and over the years he improved as an electrician.

After years of working indoors, Jake liked being out in the elements—the blistering summers, the winter days that started off at seventy then dropped to twenty with a forty mile per hour north wind, the sudden spring hail storms, the floods and droughts. The years on the lot dulled his gray eyes and weathered his face to a scowl; the street life he encountered each day sharpened his nerves.

Really, Jake thought, although Cruz looked pretty wild in his baggy gang pants and his illustrated-man tattoos, he was not that unusual. So Jake wrote off the magic-coin man as simply another character—not too different from the lost souls he encountered at the car wash from time to time: the abused young woman begging for bus fare, the deranged man who threatened Jake with a machete, the crack cocaine addicts pleading for coins, the occasional prostitute, the stream of hobos, bums, drunks and confused persons. Car wash life was the street life, and anything could happen on the street.

Jake finished cleaning up the lot, set the alarm, locked the barred doors that protected his equipment room and bill changers, and drove home.

He lived on the edge of Westcliff, near Granbury Road and Seminary Drive. It was a good house, close to Jake's job at Paschal and near to TCU where Lucy had worked in the admissions office. But now the house was getting old, and after Lucy's death, Jake had let the place go. After all, there was no one to impress, no kids, no grandkids, no nephews or nieces, and Jake had lived there so long that the neighbors forgave his ways. The gray paint was faded inside and out, the yard needed mowing, and the burglar bars were rusting away. There was a handgun in each room, a shotgun behind the front door, and thousands of dollars in quarters stacked up in the room Jake called his "office." He hadn't felt like banking lately, even though he knew it was dangerous to let the money pile up. It was possible, Jake thought as he eyed all those buckets of uncounted quarters, that the "magic" coin was still there.

With Lucy dead, Jake shared the house with an old hound, a gray, long-furred dog named Dutch that he and Lucy had found dumped at the car wash fourteen years back. Dutch slept most of the day, and at night he stayed with Jake, at the foot of the bed Jake had shared with Lucy for so long, listening, as the dog had always done, for anyone foolish enough to attempt a break in. Jake had made it his raison d'être to outlive the old dog.

Jake fixed the hound some supper, counted enough coin to stock the changers the next day, took a shower, turned on the TV, and fell asleep after drinking a beer. He had completely forgotten Cruz and the magic coin.

Cruz hadn't forgotten. He was at the lot—with his gangster buddies—the next afternoon, waiting for Jake to arrive in his old pickup. Although he had plenty of money, Jake dressed in rags and drove an old Ford truck to keep the customers from thinking it would be worth their while to mug him. It had worked for years, but Jake always carried a .32 auto in his pocket, just in case.

It was 104 degrees, and Cruz was shirtless; his tattoos swam under a glaze of sweat as he spoke.

"Find my coin, man."

Jake sensed a threat.

"I asked about it." Jake glanced at the car full of gangsters who were eyeing him. "But I don't think the owner can find it."

Cruz stared at Jake for a moment, as if he were considering what to do next.

"You tell that guy I need to talk to him. He had better give me back my coin. It's my magic, our symbol."

"Well, I can ask again, that's all I can do."

"You tell him to give me back my coin or there will be trouble."

Cruz turned and walked to his car; he and his friends talked a moment and then stared hard at Jake as they pulled off the lot and sped away with a squealing of tires. Jake noticed that the rear window of the Impala had etching on it: "Heads I Win. Tails You Lose."

At home that evening, after he fed Dutch and satisfied his thirst with a tall brew, Jake began counting coins. Counting was a chore that was never really completed—and Jake was glad of that—because it meant that business was steady. The money had stacked up for weeks, but Jake was tired, and he only ran a couple of buckets through the counting machine, looking all the while for the "magic" coin. There was an occasional slug and several quarters with holes drilled through them—a vain attempt to cheat the machines by attaching a string or wire to the quarter, but there were no "magic" coins, no coins with naked women on them.

Jake supposed that he could visit every porno-video shop in town, looking for the "Heads I Win. Tails You Lose" coin, but he couldn't do that. Lucy had declared those places off limits the day they had married, and he wasn't about to break one of her rules, even now that she had been gone for two years. Besides, Fort Worth's rogue sheriff, a fundamentalist Christian who had established a "God Pod" in the county jail, had closed down most of the porno video shops anyway.

"To hell with the magic man and the coin with the naked girl."

Dutch watched him bag another thousand in quarters.

"Do you know about honor, about magic?" Cruz demanded. "If the magic goes bad, or if you lose your honor, things go wrong."

Jake listened patiently; what else could he do? The "magic" man came by every afternoon and waited, with his unsavory pals, so he could ask again about the "magic" coin.

"I don't think we're going to find your coin. It's probably in the bank by now."

"Listen, if my luck changes, so does yours."

Cruz's tattoos gleamed purple in the deadly 109 degree sunlight.

Jake took a rag from his back pocket and wiped the sweat from his face.

"Look fellow, I don't want trouble. If you think a machine cheated you, I can give you a refund."

Cruz snorted and spit and Jake could see the anger rise in his eyes. Then Cruz turned and joined his friends who were waiting near the low-rider Chevy. The gangsters consulted a minute, climbed into their Chevy, and sped down the street.

Jake let his hand slide into his right front pants pocket where he carried his .32 auto. The fully loaded gun—eight shots of hollow-pointed power resting behind a double-action trigger—made him feel better. That was magic okay, he thought, deciding that from then on he would also carry a .38 revolver in a waist-band holster, as if the two pistols were the charms needed to protect him against the curse of a mad, "magic" man. He locked up the door to the equipment room and went home, sure that the gangsters would destroy something that night.

Much to Jake's surprise when he returned the next morning, the wash seemed undamaged: no graffiti, no cut hoses, no smashed vending machines. But inside the equipment room Jake discovered that the float valve on his hot-water holding tank had broken; three inches of water flooded the floor.

For a moment Jake looked at the flooded equipment room and considered how easy it would be to make a mistake, to accidentally touch one of the 220 wires while standing ankle-deep in water. The big shock would take him out, instantly. That was sure to be better than what happened to Lucy. He stood at the doorway, considering his move, until Lucy's voice rang out in his mind: "No!"

So he stepped back, used the wooden handle of a broom to clear the debris from the floor drain, and watched the flood recede.

Cruz did not appear that day. The temperature soared to 107. It was the fifty-third day in a row without rain.

The next morning, Dutch moved a little slow and was not interested in sharing Jake's breakfast, very unusual. And Jake too, feeling slightly off, ate only half of his eggs and toast.

Again, nothing was destroyed at the lot. There wasn't even any gang graffiti to indicate that Cruz and his buddies were interested in the place. But mechanical problems seemed to pop up everywhere: two vac motors down, a busted low pressure pump on the tire cleaner, strange wiring problems that took forever to trace. It was as if the car wash gods were angry.

"Must be that curse Cruz put on me," Jake thought.

The problems were, no doubt, related to heat stress. After all, in the summer months, temperatures inside the equipment room could reach 130 degrees Fahrenheit. There was nothing magic about it. No, Jake thought, there would be no magic for him, thank you, only electricity, physics, and sweat. That's what really keeps the world going, no matter what the New Age shamans might claim. No matter what Cruz, with his gang buddies, his "magic coin," and his swarming tattoos might think. You live, you work, you die, and if you're a little bit fortunate, as he had been with Lucy, you love a little. Nothing very magic in that, only the normal course of human existence, Jake philosophized as he methodically repaired each vac and fixed the low-pressure pump.

The vet's office was adjacent to the car wash, but years ago the vet built a tall fence around his lot to protect his employees (they had to walk the dogs that were kenneled) from Jake's customers. The vet was a bony fellow with a shock of carrot-colored hair that always needed trimming. He had treated Dutch from the day that Lucy and Jake found the poor, abandoned pup.

"I don't see anything, but he's getting really old. Let's give him a cortisone shot and half an aspirin. I'd hate to have to put him down."

The vet's comment scared Jake. That night, the second night in a row, Dutch wouldn't eat. That night the kitchen nearly caught on fire. Jake was always worried about fire. You had to worry about fire when every door and window in your house was barred shut.

It wasn't a major blaze, only a pan of bacon grease that flamed and smoked while Jake worried about the hound, but Jake had to use both of his fire extinguishers and evacuate the house, Dutch in his arms, while the smoke cleared.

As the week went by, Dutch recovered his appetite, then towards the weekend, the busiest days of a car wash week, he relapsed. Jake was determined not to take the dog back into the vet's; he was afraid of what the doctor might recommend. So he made the hound a special bed in the back room where he counted the coins. Jake counted and counted and counted until, finally, all but one bucket of quarters had been sacked into the thousand dollar bags he would deliver to the bank. He had put the chore off too long, he realized. Determined to finish counting all the coins he had collected, Jake dug into the last bucket of quarters. To his surprise, his first handful of quarters included not one, but two of the "magic" coins. They were nearly the size of a quarter, but they were tinted gold, and each coin featured the naked woman with the "Heads I Win" and the "Tails You Lose" expression.

"At last. Maybe now that bastard will leave me alone."

He fingered the coins, turning them both over and over and over in his palm.

After looking though the papers that stacked up on his desk, Jake gave up trying to find Cruz's phone number. He put the coins in the ashtray of the pickup truck so he could give them to Cruz the next time the gangsters appeared. But Jake didn't see the low riders at the wash that day, or the next, or the next, and the hound continued to grow weaker.

Then they were there, parked in the drive, admiring Jake's house, when Jake pulled up. For a change, the gangsters were all wearing shirts, identical black pullovers.

Jake was out of the truck in an instant; his hand was in his pocket, gripping the .32 auto.

"What are you doing here?"

"Came to see if you found our coin yet."

"How did you find my house?"

Cruz snorted, but he didn't smile.

"It wasn't hard. Lots of people watch you." He nodded toward Jake's home. "Lots of people knows your place—Fort Knox of Fort Worth."

"Yeah, well, I have your coin."

Without turning his back on Cruz and his gang, Jake fetched one of the gold coins from the truck's ashtray.

"Is this what you're looking for?"

Cruz examined the coin carefully, inspecting both sides before passing it on to his amigos.

"That's it. What took you so long to find it?"

"Like I told you, I don't count the stuff. The guy that owns the wash found it. I've been carrying it around hoping I'd run into you."

"You're a lucky man," Cruz said. "You don't want to know."

"Yeah, sure. Now leave me be."

Cruz and his buddies got into the Impala and sped off toward Berry Street. That was the last Jake ever saw of them; they never returned to the lot or to the house.

The next morning, Dutch was better, hungry and more active. During the week, the dog got stronger and stronger. And, almost magically, the equipment at the wash seemed to run smoother. The bums, prostitutes, and druggies seemed to disappear from the lot, and it even rained, dropping the temperature into the seventies, at least for a few hours.

When he was certain that Dutch had fully recovered, Jake took all the coins in the house—twenty-five of the thousand-dollar bags—loaded them into the back of his pickup and delivered them to the humane society on Lancaster. He left the quarters with the director—an anonymous donation.

And from that day on, Jake carried two things in his pocket: the .32 auto and the magic coin.

The Bridge at Mountainberg

Iwatched Woody as he worked the wheel and floated the pickup truck in and out of the tight curves. It was becoming a long trip, and I was already tired of the mountain roads. They were burying Doug Benson in a very inconvenient corner of the state.

"At least it's over for him now," Woody said.

Woody kept his eyes on the road. He was only about thirty, but he had lost a lot of his hair, and he looked too distinguished in his dark gray funeral suit to be what he was: shop teacher at the high school in Mountainberg, Arkansas.

"The doctors knew they couldn't help Doug. They were only keeping him alive for the insurance money."

Woody nodded in agreement. "I never did see anybody hurt that bad before."

I had worked with Doug Benson for a year. He coached football at Mountainberg, and when I first met him, I never guessed that he was sick. Doug was a wide-shouldered, big-muscled jock who was always talking about football, white-water canoeing, and young women, usually in that order.

Doug had always called me Sammy. It was "Sammy, run the team a couple of miles," or "Sammy, see that we get a bus that has a working heater for the ride to Hog Eye," or "Sammy, let's grab a brew in Fayetteville after the game."

It was kind of funny because nobody else called me that, not Woody or any of my family. I was plain Sam to everyone except Doug Benson.

Woody and Doug were already best buddies when I arrived at Mountainberg ready to teach my students all about physical education and social studies. I loved my P.E. classes. I was born to coach. But I felt a little funny about teaching social studies, you know, all that man and society stuff. I only took it in college because it was easier than math or English. Social studies was a fuzzy subject for most of the kids in my class too. Hell, if Margaret Mead herself landed in Mountainberg, the only society she'd find would be the Friday night football game and the Sunday church supper.

Anyway, I guess it was only natural for Doug, Woody, and me to hang out together. We were all still single, and compared to the other teachers at Moutainberg—most of them were so old that they'd had time to be born twice—we were still pretty young.

In fact, Doug had just turned twenty-five when he died.

I spent my first month at Mountainberg wondering why they had ever hired me since Doug was already coaching all the students there were to coach. Mountainberg never placed first in its division, but at least the football team never placed last. To tell the truth, I thought Doug was doing pretty good with the material he had to work with. Later, when Woody told me that Doug had cancer, I figured it out.

All through the fall semester, Doug and I taught our classes in the morning, and in the afternoon we gave the team the workout and watched the cheerleaders as they practiced. And every weekend, as soon as we got the Friday night game out of the way, me and Doug and Woody would meet in Fayetteville. Fayetteville was only twenty miles up the highway, but it was a world away from our little town. The state university is in Fayetteville, and those Ozark coeds are known from one end of Arkansas to the other for their fun-loving ways. And Doug, he always seemed to prove that the reputation was well-deserved.

"Boys," Doug would tell me and Woody as we sipped our Monday morning coffee and watched the high schoolers pour into the building by the bus load, "there's nothing like the dying football-hero line to charm them college gals out of their Hog sweaters."

But by spring, Doug stopped joking about his illness. He faded from one-eighty to a hundred and thirty pounds, and he was losing his thick brown hair to chemotherapy. His face was pale and thin with pain.

"The kids on the team sure loved him."

"Yeah," I agreed. "Doug was too easy on them."

I had already decided to toughen up the team with heavier practice sessions now that I was head coach.

"You know what Doug told me?"

"What?"

"He said dying was like jumping off a bridge and not knowing if you would hit rocks or water."

I was a little surprised that Woody appreciated the poetry in the statement. Woody was one-hundred percent good ol' boy; big, friendly and completely satisfied with himself. In the spring his students made metal ashtrays. In the fall they fashioned wooden Christmas presents for their parents. Woody spent his spare time drinking beer, chasing skirts, and shooting whatever species of local wildlife happened to be in season.

"I don't think dying scared Doug much," I said.

"No, Doug wasn't afraid of dying. He was afraid of pain."

Woody slowed down as we drove through the town of

Cotter. A banner strung across the main street welcomed us to the "Trout Fishing Capital of the World." We paused for the blinking traffic light in the middle of town, and when we reached the bridge that crossed the White River, Woody turned off the highway and parked the truck.

We got out of the truck and walked to the riverside. Below us the gin-clear river moved slowly, and we could easily see the trout dart through the water.

"Doug and me used to fish right down there." Woody pointed to a rocky shoal. "He caught a ten-pound rainbow half a mile up river from here."

Woody stared at the moving water a minute and shook his head. "Doug liked fishing better than anything. He always said that the trout were the only good thing to come from damming up this river. The water comes from the bottom of the lake now—too cold for anything except trout."

We watched a large, silvery fish swim past.

"You mean that's the only kind of fish left in the river?"

"That's right. When they first opened the gates, cold water killed out everything. The river was dead until they put the trout in. They still can't get the rainbows to breed here. Seems like the trout know something's wrong, that they don't really belong."

Then Woody reached into the pocket of his suit coat and took out a plastic pill bottle. He twisted off the cap and dropped pills into the water. There were red pills, green pills, capsules and tablets of all shapes and colors. When he was finished, he threw the bottle in and watched it float down-stream and disappear.

Woody didn't say a thing, so I followed him back to the truck. We got in and drove across the bridge; the wide river was a sheen of smooth, flowing water below.

"You're most likely wondering what was going on back

there."

Woody drove faster to make up for lost time.

"It caught my attention all right."

"That was Doug's secret supply. For a long time he skimped on his pain pills, hoarded up a bunch of them. Told me he was saving up for the time when he really needed them."

Woody shot me a "you know" look and stopped talking long enough to swing us around a slow moving tractor pulling a load of hay.

"Anyway, the last time Doug went into the hospital, he made me promise to give him his pills if his pain got so bad that he couldn't stand it anymore."

I stared out the window and watched the soft, sun-soaked hills roll by. To tell the truth, I was a little ashamed that I had only gone to visit Doug once during all the time that he was in the hospital. I hadn't stayed long then because his sister from Joplin came by, and I figured they wanted to be alone.

"Yeah, the last time I saw him he looked at me with those glazed eyes. I could tell the morphine wasn't cutting the pain for him. I sat down by him. He asked me for his pills. He'd had enough, I guess, and wanted to get it done."

Woody lit a cigarette.

"I had the pills with me. I could have left them next to his water. But instead I told him I'd have to go home to get them. Then I went straight to Rodger's Bar and got drunk. When I went back to the hospital the next day, they told me Doug had died during the night. I should have given him the pills."

I didn't know what Woody should have done, and I didn't know what to say, so I was glad to see a road sign pointing toward Doug's hometown, a placed called Fifty-Six.

Fifty-Six might have been the population of the town. It was nothing but an intersection on the highway with a few mobile homes and shacks scattered about the hills. We followed the directions Doug's folks had given us and turned off on a farm-to-market road.

"That must be it." Woody pointed to a mobile home with about a hundred cars parked in front.

We soon found out that the entire Benson clan had assembled for Doug's funeral. I remembered Doug's sister. She was a good-looking girl who worked in Joplin. She introduced Woody and me to Doug's mother, a thin, red-headed woman who must have been pretty before time and country life wore her down. She had lost most of her sight, but she could still see well enough to get around the house and the yard. Doug's father greeted Woody and me with a firm handshake, but he had been wounded in Korea and had trouble hobbling around even with the help of a walker.

After we ate our fill of fried chicken, mashed potatoes, and green beans, Doug's mother led Woody and me out behind the trailer and pointed to two apple trees.

"You boys see them trees?"

It was like she needed to be reassured that they were still there.

"Yes'm," Woody answered.

"Doug planted them trees when he was ten years old. He watered them 'most every day until he went to college. Those trees give plenty of apples, good sweet ones, too."

Then it was time for the service. Woody and I got into the pickup and followed the others up the road to the hill where Doug was being buried in the Benson plot. The hillside was covered with tall, burnt-brown grass that waved in the hot wind, but inside the cemetery, all the graves were green and well-trimmed.

There must have been two-hundred people, including most of the members of the Mountainberg High football team and a half a dozen cute coeds from Fayetteville. All the old folks were trying to squeeze into the shade of a single oak tree that stood in the middle of the graveyard. A tractor was parked outside the fence that separated the cemetery from the pasture where cattle grazed. A man wearing a sweat-soaked tee-shirt smoked a cigarette beside the tractor and waited for us to finish so he could fill in the grave and escape the heat.

The undertaker made a joke about how light the coffin was as Woody and me took our places as pallbearers, and after we helped carry the coffin from the hearse to the grave, the preacher, a fat fellow who looked to be about fifty, started his speech.

"Good people," he said as a drop of sweat rolled down his cheek, "we are here today to honor a fallen hero. You all knew Doug Benson. Doug Benson was a fighter. He was a fighter on the playing field, a fighter for young minds in his classroom, and a fighter to the end with his battle against cancer. Doug proved his heroism every day. Doug Benson suffered, but he never gave in. He showed us all, showed us with his dignity in the face of pain and by the intensity of his will to live, how precious this thing we call life is."

The preacher used his handkerchief to dab the sweat from his forehead. Then he continued the service.

"In some way or another, Doug touched all of us."

The preacher wiped his forehead again, and one of the coeds fought back a smile.

"Many of the young people Doug worked with are here today. I know that Doug's family was especially proud that Doug had become a teacher, a model for the young in this troubled time. Each of us will miss Doug Benson. But we can all be assured that Doug's gone on, on to a place where there is no pain and where there is no death. Doug Benson's gone on now, as we will all go on, if only we believe in life everlasting in Jesus' name."

The preacher drifted off into a long prayer while I looked down into the neatly cut hole in the earth. Then the preacher finished, and everybody stared real hard at me and Woody and the other pallbearers as we lowered Doug into the ground. Doug's mother broke into a fit of sobbing and had to be helped away as the undertaker turned on a tape player and "Shall We Gather at the River" floated over the mourners and the wide-eyed cattle that had wandered up to the fence.

When the service was over, Woody and I turned away from the grave and started back to the pickup truck. All during our silent drive back to Mountainberg, I prayed for Doug Benson, for myself, for all of us, hoping that when we jumped from that bridge we hit water, not rock.

No Scars Whatsoever

Danger! Danger! Danger! The alarm flashed in Matt's mind the moment Kelly rolled off of him, stretched her young body, and said, "Oh, baby! That was the best ever." While Kelly had always been a bit of a savage in the sack, she wasn't known—at least to Matt—to be overly generous in her reviews. And he knew from experience to expect trouble whenever something tripped his mental early warning system.

The evening began in an ordinary fashion. They had dated for three years, they had been engaged for eighteen months, and they followed a clearly established ritual. It was Saturday, so Matt worked till noon, and after he got off work, he drove to Kelly's apartment on the northwest side of Houston. He and Kelly would swim, play tennis, or, if the weather was bad, watch a video. Then Matt drove the thirty minutes of freeway to his own apartment where he showered and dressed and then hurried back to Kelly's place.

They went to dinner at their favorite restaurant, a grill on Airline Drive called the Bar-B-Que Inn. There was always a noisy, beery crowd in the place, and everyone seemed to know that the seafood was better than the brisket. Kelly wore a white dress with a red belt, and the dress seemed to make her brown hair darker. Her eyes—which usually seemed like blue ice to Matt—flashed in the dim light as if there were a fire smoldering within them.

But other than the new dress and the strange look in Kelly's eyes, nothing seemed out of the ordinary about the evening, nothing except that Kelly consumed most of a bottle of Dry Creek Fumé along with her dinner of flounder stuffed with crab meat. When they finished their meal, they drove the freeway back to Kelly's apartment, passing the fenced-off luxury hotels and the boarded-up office buildings as they drove. No, there had been nothing in the evening to warn Matt that he was in for either trouble or great sex, nothing until Kelly's praise tripped the alarm in his head.

Funny, Matt thought, funny to think about sex in such terms: the great, the good, the mediocre. Maybe the sex had been great, and he had simply been too overwhelmed to realize it. Maybe, like vacations and childhood, this sex would seem better in retrospect. Matt had to admit that he loved the way Kelly moaned. There was something delicious about the low rasp of her voice as she let out long syllables of pleasure. It was as if she were urging herself on to a finish line that only she could see in a race that only she could run. Kelly made noise part of the experience, and judging from the decibel level that night, Kelly had won a marathon.

The trouble came when she caught her breath and lit her after-intercourse cigarette.

"Honey, I had a discussion with the doctor the other day, and we've decided that it's time for me to quit the pill."

The danger alarm flashed again in Matt's mind.

"Well, what's the problem?"

"It's not wise to smoke and take the pill."

"You could quit smoking."

"Sure." Kelly took another puff. "Or I could give up sex."

"You don't have anything else in mind?"

"The doctor suggested several alternatives. I've got another appointment with him."

Matt got up from the bed and put on his trousers. This was just like her. She would never come out and say, "I want to have a baby." No, she would never be that direct. With Kelly it always had to be a plan, a scheme, a way to get exactly what she wanted without having to say exactly what that was. In some ways Kelly was the opposite of Matt. Matt never planned anything; his teachers had always marked the "acts before thinking" column on his report cards. Kelly never did anything on impulse; she plotted every move she made as if her life were a game of chess.

"I always thought the pill was the best. But I guess, if anything happened, you could have an—"

"No, I'd never do that." Kelly cut him off. "You know I've always thought that was wrong."

Matt found his shirt, put it on, and fumbled with the buttons.

"I guess we could use condoms like everybody else."

"They're not really all that reliable, are they?"

"Not really."

The fact was that Matt despised condoms. He was happy that he had found Kelly, happy that they loved one another and that they had been able to escape the not-so-wonderful world of latex. Where was the spontaneity in an act that started with putting on a glove? Yes, Matt thought, a disease- infested world made monogamy and marriage an alluring option.

Kelly was still in bed, naked on top of the white sheet, her long brown hair spilling out onto the pillows behind her head. Matt looked at her bronzed body and realized that she was working on her seamless tan again, doing some topless sunbathing on the balcony of her apartment.

"Did the doctor mention that I could have myself fixed, you know, a vasectomy?"

Matt gave her an inquiring glance and wondered how she would sidestep the suggestion.

Kelly leaned across the bed and put out her cigarette in the ashtray on the nightstand.

"No." She took a long time to fish another cigarette out of the pack. "What if we want to have kids later? And besides, I guess he didn't think of that because I'm still single. Not all of us single girls sleep with one guy, you know."

"Yeah, I know." Matt looked her in the eyes when she turned to face him. "But I like it this way."

"So do I."

But she wasn't smiling, and neither was he. She lit another cigarette and allowed a cloud of blue smoke to hang over the bed like an omen.

The freeway was especially jammed on Monday. Since he was only moving three miles an hour, Matt had plenty of time to think over his situation. The mirrored-glass office buildings—many of them sporting "For Sale" or "For Lease" signs on their overgrown lawns—reflected Matt's old Ford pickup as it inched along the expressway. The recession of '81 had started when Matt moved to Houston, and even three years later, there was still a lot of vacant real estate. Matt was lucky to have a job; many didn't. But it seemed to him as if the traffic jam was another chain around his life, a chain like working in the "cage" or like being married with children or like owning a house. "That's how they get you," he said to himself. "One link at a time."

He glanced at his watch. The gridlock was likely to make him late for work. He turned on the radio and tuned in the oldie-goldie Western station. Although most of the music the station played was older than he was, it was the only music he liked. All the songs seemed so simple and free. Kelly hated old music; all she would listen to was new country—love songs by pretty cowboys. Matt detested newer country music, but most of the time he kept quiet and let Kelly have her way about the choice of stations. He knew he would never change her.

Matt was the oldest child in his family; he had two brothers and two sisters. His father had left when Matt was ten, and he had helped care for the younger children after his mother had become ill. When his mother had died, his younger brothers and sisters moved to El Paso to live with an aunt and uncle. Matt finished high school, fled the small west Texas town of Pecos, and took a job in Houston. He wanted to be on his own, wanted to try living in the city. That seemed like a long time ago to him now.

Finally he reached his exit, swung off the expressway, and made up for lost time by speeding down the four lane boulevard toward Brenda Avenue, where Weather-Rite occupied one of the warehouses that lined the street. Matt had worked at Weather-Rite for nearly four years. When he first arrived in Houston, he answered a newspaper ad for a warehouse worker and hired on at the air conditioning and heating wholesale distributorship.

He started out working in the warehouse, driving a fork lift and loading trucks with condensing units, coils, and furnaces. He advanced from fork-lift driver to counter sales in the parts department, where he remained. Weather-Rite made a lot of money selling repair parts; motors, switches, and transformers were all marked up a hundred per cent to the retailers who would then mark them up two hundred per cent before selling them to home owners. Matt was good at parts; he memorized most of the air conditioner and heater models in the catalog and organized the parts room so that he could locate nearly anything without a lot of effort. Matt figured that Mr. Marcus, Kelly's uncle and owner of Weather- Rite, would be happy to allow him to work the "cage" as long as Weather-Rite was in business.

Matt met Kelly at Weather-Rite the summer after she graduated from high school; Mr. Marcus had hired his niece as a secretary. She moved on to a position with CompuTex, the computer manufacturing company.

Marcus was an obese, happy fellow who loved his black Lincoln Town Car and who thought no one knew that he was gay. He was a planner, a plotter like his niece. Matt suspected that Marcus and Kelly had everything figured out. Matt and Kelly would marry; then Kelly could run the office, Matt could sell the air conditioners, and Uncle Marcus could spend more time in Acapulco with his vivacious friends. Then, in about thirty or so years, Kelly and Matt could hand the business over to their kids. Matt had nothing against marriage and family, not if such developments existed in some remote future, but thinking about such things as immediate possibilities was enough to trip Matt's alarm, so he forced the thoughts from his mind as he pulled into the Weather-Rite parking lot.

He eased into his assigned place, looked at himself in the rear-view, and decided his short, black hair didn't need combing. There was a chance of rain that day, so Mr. Marcus had parked his Town Car inside the warehouse. Marcus had a theory that the Houston rain was so polluted that it would hurt the finish of his car. He even went so far as to pull off the road and park under bridges during rain storms. People made fun of Marcus for taking such good care of his Lincoln, but everyone agreed that the Houston air was deadly. The freeways were lined with dying pine trees.

Matt got out of his truck and walked up the steps to the side door of Weather-Rite. No matter what happened between him and Kelly, Matt knew that he didn't intend to spend the next thirty years of his life inside the "cage" with Bub Johnson.

Johnson was already there, huddled over his desk with his ear to the phone in the dim corner of the parts cage. He was fifteen years older than Matt, and ten of those years belonged to Weather-Rite. Bub was a lean six-foot-two-inches tall, and he dressed in scuffed cowboy boots and a brown uniform that had Weather-Rite embroidered above the shirt pocket. He looked like your everyday redneck except that he wore his long gray hair tied in a ponytail.

Matt and Bub called their office the "cage" because their work area was really nothing more than a fenced-in corner of the warehouse with a counter running down one side. The cage was one of Mr. Marcus's ideas.

"Why spend money putting in walls?" Marcus rested his hands on his belly as if he were trying to get the huge lunch he had consumed to settle down. "Put a chain link fence around this corner of the warehouse so the customers can't steal anything. We'll put up shelves and this will be our parts department."

And that's exactly what Mr. Marcus did. A chain fence ran around three sides of the room, and a chest-high counter secured the forth side. Mr. Marcus installed some lights, ran some extra phone lines, and moved in a couple of desks to complete the room. There was no air conditioning and little heating, and except for the annual change of light bulbs and calendars, the cage remained the same for years. When the customers teased Matt and Bub about their work place, Bub would always say that chain link did not a prison make, but Matt wasn't so sure of that.

Bub hung up the phone, went over to the coffee maker, and poured coffee into a "Houston Oilers" cup.

"Hope you got something sweet from Kelly this morning because you'll need to be in a good mood to survive this day."

Matt sat down at his desk.

"What's up?"

"Special inventory. Some big shot accounting firm's going to supervise it. Word is they were sent down by the bank."

"Great."

Bub had been right. The day was awful. Matt hated taking inventory more than anything else; the usual twice-a-year was enough as far as he was concerned. And the junior accountants in their clean white shirts and seventy-dollar ties hadn't been much of a help. They spent the entire day doodling on their clipboards and dabbing the sweat from their brows with their silk handkerchiefs while Bub and Matt were on hands and knees, counting every o-ring and every transformer in every bin.

But business had been slow for a summer day, and Bub and Matt had completed the chore by 8:30 that evening. When Matt finally got to his apartment, there was a message from Kelly on his recorder.

"Honey, I called you at work, but Uncle Marcus said you were busy doing inventory. Listen. Things are so slow at CompuTex that they asked if anyone could take an unpaid leave. I decided this would be a good chance for me to drive up to Oklahoma and visit mother. I'm leaving this afternoon, so I'll call you later. Pick up my mail and water the house plants. I love you, baby. Bye now."

Danger! Danger! Danger! The alarm tripped again in

Matt's head. But what was dangerous about Kelly going to Oklahoma to visit her mother? He couldn't help but have a vague suspicion that Kelly, her mother, and her uncle were conspiring against him. A chill ran through him, but he quickly shook it off. No, he thought. He was only being silly.

Bub handed Matt a bottle of beer.

"So she picked up and left for Oklahoma?"

It was Saturday afternoon, and with Kelly out of town, Matt had a chance to visit Bub and his family: Meg and the three kids. Bub often asked Matt and Kelly to come for dinner, but Kelly didn't really like Bub all that much, and she hated the drive out to his mobile home. Bub lived on the far northwest outskirts of the Houston metroplex. It took him an hour to drive to work and another hour to drive home, but the reward for the commute was impressive: a two-acre stand of pines with no neighbors visible.

"Yeah. That's right. And she hasn't called me yet. I'm getting a little worried."

Bub nodded and leaned back in his lawn chair in an attempt to see the tops of the pines

Bub was on his second marriage. Wife number one had left Bub with a stack of bills to pay and a two-year-old son to raise. Meg was a major improvement. She was a thin redhead with a regular job as a cashier at a supermarket. She took good care of Bub and his son, as well as the two children she brought with her from her first marriage. It seemed to Matt that all Meg ever did was work, either at the store or at home taking care of Bub and the kids.

While Bub and Matt were outside sipping brews, Meg was busy in the kitchen frying up a mess of catfish. The three children were somewhere in the woods playing hide and seek.

"Things have been sort of strained between me and Kelly lately," Matt confessed.

Bub took a sip of beer but didn't say anything. Bub took everything in stride. Nothing seemed to upset him, not his job, not his wife, not his kids.

"You ever think how different things would be if you weren't married? I mean if you'd never had kids? You know, I mean how free you'd be and all?"

Bub smiled.

"I thought about that stuff a lot after my first marriage broke up. It's only natural to look at what you've done and wonder how things might have turned out. It was tough on me before I met Meg. I mean trying to raise a kid on my own and all."

"I don't know." Matt finished off his beer.

"You've got cold feet, is all. There's not a man alive who wouldn't get a little nervous about the prospect of getting married and settling down. But it's not so bad, not if you got a good woman to help you out."

Matt couldn't think of anything to say.

"The problem is that you're fighting it." Bub waved his beer bottle through the air. "It's something that happens to you, like it says on the bumper sticker. Look at me. I'm happy. Living in this trailer house, working my ass off in the cage. It don't mean a thing so long as I got Meg and the kids."

Matt was thinking this over when Meg opened the front door of the trailer to tell them that dinner was nearly ready. She wiped her hands on her apron.

"Honey, see if you can round up the kids. Supper won't be long now."

Meg returned to the kitchen as the three children came running out of the woods.

"Daddy! Daddy!" the girl yelled. "Make them stop!"

The two boys were chasing their younger sister, and the older boy had a dead snake draped over a stick. The little girl was a redhead, a small version of Meg with a terrorized look in her eyes. Bub got up from his lawn chair, walked over to the little girl, and scooped her up into his arms.

"I've warned you boys about playing too rough with your sister. Now get rid of that thing and go get cleaned up." He put the girl back down. "Your mom has supper ready."

The boys hung their heads and muttered, "Yes, sir." The older one returned the dead snake to the woods then shuffled into the mobile home. Bub got another beer out of the ice chest, sat back down in his lawn chair, and popped the top on the brew.

"Nope. It don't get no better than this."

There was another message from Kelly on the recorder when Matt returned home.

"Darling," Kelly said in her slow, raspy voice, "I'm sorry I keep missing you. Listen. I'm taking mother to a specialist in Oklahoma City. I don't think it's serious, so don't worry. I'm not sure where we'll be staying, but we'll be back in a couple of days, and I'll call you then. Love you. Bye."

The alarm tripped again, but Matt fought the panic, and the danger flag vanished from his mind.

He brushed his teeth, put on his pajamas, and climbed into bed to watch the ten o'clock news. He fell asleep during the nightly body count, but his dreams were unsettling, full of screaming children and a wife named Kelly who had grown fat. He dreamed that they all—Kelly, him, and the ten children—lived in the cage with Uncle Marcus.

He woke in a sweat the next morning, made a pot of

coffee, and opened the yellow pages of the phone book to the physician section. Somewhere out there was an urologist who could prevent his nightmare from becoming a reality. He would take care of this while Kelly was away. Then, when she returned, he would tell her what he had done. If she still wanted to marry him, fine. If not, well, he would worry about that later.

There were lots of urologists in the Houston phone book, too many in fact. Then a name struck Matt's fancy: Dr. Rick Risk. Matt decided to give Dr. Risk a call. After all, Matt reasoned, you had to be good to stay in the urology business with a name like Risk. And besides, there was the thrill of gambling in the name. Why not take a risk on Dr. Risk? Why not, indeed?

When Matt first visited with Dr. Risk, the worry alarm sounded; Matt imagined that it would be difficult to convince the doctor to perform the surgery. But there was no problem at all. Dr. Risk was a short, trim man about forty years old with a bushy gray mustache. The doctor explained the procedure: the cutting of the vas deferens, the blocking of the sperm ducts, the fact that everything else would work as well as usual. ("Or maybe even better than before.") Matt would need only a few days off work to recuperate after the surgery.

"At this time," Dr. Risk explained, "the government has set no rules concerning who may have this operation, so long as they are at least twenty-one years of age. You've probably heard that the procedure can be reversed, but don't count on that. The reversal is painful and expensive and doesn't always work. But if you are sure you want a vasectomy, I promise you, it's a safe and simple operation that leaves no scars whatsoever."

"Really? I mean after the stitches are taken out there

will be no sign of the surgery?"

"Oh, there will be some redness around the incision for a while. But he cuts are very small, and any redness will quickly fade away."

"I've made up my mind."

"Fine." Dr. Risk smiled. "Now, about my fee? Will you be using insurance?"

"I'll be paying cash."

Mr. Marcus sat behind his desk with a perplexed look on his round face and with his hands folded over his big belly.

"No, I don't know what could be wrong with Kelly's mother. You say they went to see a specialist?"

"That's what the message said."

"I'm curious about it too. But I guess we'll find out what's going on in due time. Now, you want to take a four-day weekend, do you? What do you have planned? Sowing a few wild oats before the wedding?"

Matt blushed.

"I need to go out to Pecos and check on that old house my mother left me. I figured it would be a good time to go, with Kelly out of town an all."

"Sure," Marcus grinned. "Take as long as you need."

"Now's the time to let me know if you want to back out." Dr. Risk waved his scalpel like a tennis racket. "I've got one of them cut, and I'm about to do the second one."

Matt opened his eyes and blinked. Fluorescent lighting always left him slightly dazed, especially when he was under the influence of a sedative and a local anesthetic. The room began to spin, the assembly-line art on the wall—really nothing more than splashes of color meant to resemble some impressionistic something—shifted in his vision then returned to a state of stability. Matt focused on the scalpel in the doctor's gloved hand.

"How about it?" The gauze mask muffled the surgeon's voice. "Meter's running, you know."

The light gleamed off of the polished steel of the scalpel. There was a flash of anxiousness in the doctor's eyes as he waited for a reply.

"Yes, yes. Go ahead."

"Good boy. I hate leaving a job half done. We won't be much longer now."

Matt felt a tightness in his groin and then a slight tugging sensation as Dr. Risk clasped the vas deferens and made his final snip.

"We've done the cutting, and now I'm tying them off. Everything looks fine. No problems."

The local was beginning to wear off, and Matt became aware of a dull soreness between his legs.

"You know, they're doing these in the bus stations in India. I've heard that the really quick surgeons can do thirty of these in an hour—one every two minutes. Not much time to reconsider there."

Matt felt a few dull tugs at his scrotum as Dr. Risk tightened the stitches. There was yet another tug, but this time the pain was sharp and clear, like a fact that defies denial.

"Almost finished now. Only a little longer."

"I think the local is wearing off."

"It's okay. We're done. And it's another fine job if I do say so myself. A fine job indeed. I give you my personal guarantee. No scars whatsoever."

"Is that it. Am I finished?"

"You're not finished," Risk joked, "but we stopped you at the starting line. Go on. You can get up now and get dressed. You're going to be a bit sore for a while, but I'll give you a prescription for some pain killers. How are you getting home?"

"By cab."

"Well, stop at the pharmacy and get the prescription filled."

Matt awkwardly climbed off of the operating chair. The soreness was spreading: a warm glow of pain that centered in his testicles and radiated through his lower body. He took off his operating gown and carefully put on his underwear, his slacks, his shirt, and his shoes. Matt was weak in the knees, and Dr. Risk had to help him walk out to the waiting room.

"You can expect a little swelling. It'll be a while before you feel up to giving us a sample." Dr. Risk handed Matt a test tube protected by a sterile plastic wrap.

"What do I do with this?"

"Collect a sample in the tube and then bring it back to me. If it tests clear, then your worries are over."

Matt went home, took two pain pills, and went to bed. When he awoke the next morning, his testicles were the size of tennis balls, and the fear alarm was sounding in his brain.

He was lying on the couch in a pain-pill stupor when Kelly called from Oklahoma.

"Honey, is everything all right there?"

Matt hesitated a moment.

"Yes, but I was getting worried about you."

"I'm fine. And Mother's fine too. I'll tell you about it when I get back."

"When will that be?"

"Well, I called CompuTex, and they said I could miss another week."

Matt cleared his throat.

"Baby, when you get home, we need to talk."
"I know. Don't worry. I'll be back soon."

As Dr. Risk had promised, the swelling and the pain vanished, and after Risk removed the stitches, Matt was feeling nearly normal. The results of his sperm count came in: zero. He tested clear. He dodged one trap. The mental alarm hadn't sounded in a while, and Matt was becoming comfortable with the choice he had made. True, he made an impulsive decision; he acted before thinking, but maybe that was for the best. After all, it would be better to lose Kelly because of what he had done than to separate later with kids to support. He would explain it all to Kelly when she returned from Oklahoma. She would have to take or leave him as he was. There would be no going back.

Things went on as usual at Weather-Rite. Bub worked the cage, Mr. Marcus pulled his Town Car into the warehouse at the slightest hint of rain, and Matt sat at his desk, staring at his parts catalog and dreaming about ways to inform Kelly about the operation. Really, Matt thought, the coward's way out would be to not tell Kelly a thing. The scars from the surgery were tiny and fading fast. By the time Kelly returned, there would be little evidence. After all, no matter how great the sex was, Kelly didn't spend an enormous amount of time inspecting his testicles.

Kelly arrived at his apartment on Sunday afternoon. She wore blue jeans and her CompuTex T-shirt, the one that had "Computer-4-U" printed across the front. She was as beautiful as ever. The only change was that she had gained a few pounds in the weeks that she had been away, and she seemed to have given up smoking. Her mother must have done a lot of cooking for her, Matt thought. He took her into his arms and held her.

"I'm glad you're back."

She pulled away from him and looked him in the eye. "I've got something to tell you."

"Me too,"

"I'm pregnant."

He stared into her ice-blue eyes.

"I knew before I left, but I didn't know what to tell you. I was afraid."

'It's okay." He took her back into his arms. "It's okay."

"Do you still want me?"

"Of course."

After a moment she asked, "What was it you wanted to tell me?"

"Nothing. Only that I love you very much."

The wedding was the next week. It was a small ceremony conducted by a justice of the peace in the offices of Weather-Rite. Matt wore his only suit, the black one he had bought for his mother's funeral, and Kelly wore her white dress with the red belt. Kelly's mother rode the bus down from Oklahoma, and Bub was there with Meg and the three kids. He gave Matt an I-told-you-so wink when Matt said "I do."

Marcus was all smiles, and, as a wedding gift, he gave Matt a set of keys to a new company car. They could use the car, Uncle Marcus said, on the honeymoon—a trip to South Padre.

After the wedding they all went out to dinner at the Bar-B-Que Inn. Matt kept waiting, listening for alarms as he and Kelly, man and wife and child-to-be, climbed into the back of Uncle Marcus's Town Car. Matt listened and listened as they sped down the freeway, but there was nothing, no alarms at all, no scars whatsoever.

Ridin' My Thumb to Mexico

Dad was big-time pissed with me that year because the university at Austin had transformed me from a "never broke a rule" highschooler to a "never follow a rule" hippie. He hated my long hair, my dope smoking, my anti-war rants, and my screwing his friends' daughters. He had recently caught me puffing on a joint out behind the parts room, and that, of course, did not help things one bit. He was probably glad I was going to spend a month in Mexico.

"Maybe after a month in Mexico, after you see how tough it is down there, you'll realize how good you have it and stop bad mouthing America."

Dad was suspiciously quiet as he drove me to the edge of the suburban metromess so I could catch my first ride. He pulled the car onto the shoulder of I-35 south of the Fort Worth-Burleson line. The radio blared more of its same sad song about Watergate and Nixon as I pulled my pack from the back seat and tossed it onto the grass. It was already ninety degrees, and heat waved off the fields beyond the interstate.

"Don't worry. I'll be back to inventory the parts before school starts."

"We won't wait up."

Dad was a real Texan, one cut from the "old rock." His great grandparents came to Texas from Germany, his father lost everything in the Depression, and Dad lied

39

about his age to enlist in the service after Pearl Harbor. He believed pot was something like heroin, that only "bad" girls had sex before marriage, and that fooling around was a dangerous step: "You keep messing with those girls," he'd say, "and you're going to get yourself shot. Or worse, you'll get one of 'em pregnant."

He had never met Christi, but he could quit worrying about facing down his buddies at church now that the object of my affection was from Waco. And even though we didn't always get along so well, I still tried to help my folks out at the family business. It was tough going, what with Mom doing the books and Dad selling stoves, range tops, vent hoods, and garbage disposals from the "showroom." But it was what we did, and the store had provided us all a living and given me a chance at college. I spent all of June organizing the parts room, sweeping floors, polishing dishwashers, saving every dime for my escape to Mexico with Christi. July was for Christi and me; I didn't want to think about August.

Even though Dad seemed cool to me on that hot morning, his eyes looked a little foggy as he wiped his glasses, glanced in the rearview, then at me and my pack, and pulled away, driving south to the next exit so he could make a turn back toward town and the store that was eating away at him and Mom. My mother wasn't very pleased with my summer plans, but Dad had said that if, as a twenty year old, he could survive a hike across Germany with people shooting at him, then I, as a twenty year old, could probably survive a month in Mexico. But since Mom was a worrier, I told her that I'd be Greyhounding, not thumbing, my way south.

Within minutes I was speeding along in the cab of a junker pickup driven by a cowboy with a hangover.

"I don't usually pick up hippies but you looked harmless enough."

He was right. I looked like what I was: a skinny, long-haired kid from the suburbs—like John Lennon without a guitar, an English accent, or wire-rimmed glasses.

He offered me a brew, which I turned down since it was nine in the morning. He was obviously one of those fellows who measured the miles across Texas in beers. The morning beer was apparently needed to steady his nerves. He looked a bit bleary eyed under his sweat-stained Rudolf's Plumbing gimme cap, and I hoped he could keep the old pickup in the right lane.

"In fact, we used to kick the shit out of hippies, you know—if we were drunk or pissed enough. Those were the days, huh?"

The cowboy shot me a sinister grin and pushed his Rudolf cap a bit to the left side of his head to block the morning sun. He turned the dial on the radio till he tuned in a station playing the number one country song of the summer of '73: "Ridin' My Thumb to Mexico" by Johnny Rodriguez. The tune reminded me of my mission.

"I guess we hated you hippie guys because most of you are rich college kids and you get all that college pussy plus draft deferments, too."

"Even college boys have draft numbers now."

"Yeah, well, maybe so. But I know you guys get laid more than eggs. All I got was a wife who turned to ice when the money ran low. Then she started messing around with some dude from work, and now she's PG'ed and I'll get to support a kid that's probably not even mine. God bless America! Let me warn you boy. You knock up one of them college chicks and that'll be the end. Then you'll be like me, paying, paying, and paying while your ex is partying every night."

"You sound like my dad."

"Listen to your father, son."

We didn't talk much the next hundred miles to Waco. The exits for the little towns clicked by, and I let the rolling, burnt-brown fields flow along to the country music on the radio. But as we pulled into Waco, a patrol car snapped up behind us, red lights flashing.

"Shit, where'd he come from?"

Rudolf tired to push the empty beer cans beneath the seat. We pulled over, and the officer appeared at the driver's window.

"I need to see a license."

The cop had a cold, professional expression. Then his nose wrinkled.

"I smell beer. Step out of the truck."

Rudolf got out of the truck and two empty beer cans bounced out behind him.

"You been drinking?"

The one thing I hated more than Nixon was the cops, and before I could stop myself, I blurted out "They're not his. They're mine."

"Is that so? Then you get out of the truck, and bring that pack with you."

The cop checked the driver's papers, then turned to me.

"You two are an odd couple."

"He was hitching. I picked him up. Next thing I knew he was pulling beers out of his pack."

"You don't even look old enough to drink."

"I'm legal."

He didn't need to know about the half ounce of pot I had in my boot.

The officer checked my license and patted me down. He made me walk the white line, but I clearly wasn't drunk. He dumped my pack and went through everything: the micro-tent, the sleeping bag, the clothes, the rain gear, the tiny backpacker's stove, the cook kit, the first aid kit, my Spanish dictionary and spare canteen of water. He knew what he was looking for, but he couldn't find it. After twenty minutes of searching, the cop gave up and let us go our way. Rudolf dropped me off in front of the McDonald's across the interstate from Baylor University, and I unloaded my pack.

"Thanks, kid. For a hippie, you're okay."

Christi and I had planned our escape for months, but I figured the odds were only fifty-fifty that she would actually show up. But there she was, standing in front of the McDonald's, dressed in a white, long sleeve shirt, faded blue jeans, and good hiking boots, pack leaning against the golden arches and hair pulled back under a straw cowgirl hat. Even in those clothes she was beautiful—five foot six, plenty of curves, chestnut hair and green eyes—and I knew I'd have no trouble getting a ride so long as Christi stood beside me. A friend dropped her off at the McDonald's because her parents would never have allowed her to ride a thumb to Mexico with me or any other boy-man. They were still spooked about what had happened in high school—the baby and all. So Christi had lied to them, told them she was going to spend a month with a girlfriend on the beach at South Padre.

I met the parents once. Her dad was a tax lawyer, tall with a thin face the color of pink granite. The house was a four bedroom ranch style on five manicured acres—a far cry from the apartment my folks had moved into to save money. "Father" led me through each room, explaining all the photos on the walls: lots of shots of him, his rifle, and dead animals with large horns.

"Got that one last year in South Africa." He smiled and

pointed to a picture of himself standing beside a downed Cape buffalo. "I would have mounted that one, but Christi's mother doesn't want a bunch of dead animals on the walls. You do any shooting?"

"Only a little pool."

It was clear that Christi had gotten her green eyes and her curves from her mother, who was kindly, but concerned. Later, I learned that when Christi told her folks, they sent her away, to Fort Worth, of all places, where she spent her senior year at the Gladney Center, waiting to deliver the baby to its adopted parents. Then her parents dispatched Christi to Guatemala—charity work. Her Spanish was nearly perfect.

I examined Christi's pack.

"We'll need to wrap that sleeping bag in your ground cloth," I said. "First rule of the road. Keep the sleeping gear dry."

"You'll have to teach me."

We crossed the bridge over the freeway to the motel that advertised, ever so discreetly, on its billboard:

Couples—$12

We spent the day playing with our gear.

Early the next morning, the soldier gave us our first ride. He was in uniform, sergeant's stripes and all, driving an older Chevy four door. Christi sat in the back seat while I got in up front.

"Name's James. I can take you to Belton. I'm going to the base in Killeen."

Killeen was the home of Fort Hood, a large base where the draftees were trained for duty.

"Thanks for stopping," Christi said.

"I've done my share of hitchin', but I never had such a pretty partner as you when I was on the road."

He looked at Christi in the rear view and gave her a wink.

"You know, a lot of military types won't talk to people like us," I said, "much less help them out or give them a ride."

"Yeah, and a lot of people like you spit on people like me—call us baby killers."

I hated Nixon and the war, but I never went that far, and I remembered the soldiers who came from Fort Hood to Austin for one of the demonstrations—GI's against the war. Feeling guilty about being safe in college while they risked everything, I let four of them stay in my dorm room. They didn't seem much like baby killers; they were victims of the draft, forced to join or be jailed. With a little less luck, I might have been one of them.

As he promised, James dropped us outside of Belton, and we were picked up in a few minutes by a red-faced, red-haired hippie named Bob who nursed his old VW van down the interstate at fifty miles an hour. A student like me and Christi, he was going to Austin to start the second session of summer school at the university. Bob fired up a joint, the sacrament of our tribe, and we passed it around.

"Why don't you two stay over at my place a couple of days? My girlfriend and me have plenty of weed, and Kinky Friedman is playing at the Armadillo."

The Armadillo World Headquarters was the cultural center of our hippie nation. A gutted National Guard armory, the Armadillo was a large tin building with a high roof and a stage at one end. It was justly famous as the home of some of the hottest music in the Southwest. In addition to hosting rock and country bands, the 'Dillo was

45

the birthplace of the odd, underground effort to establish the armadillo as the official state animal of Texas. In fact, a local artist recently painted a mural on one side of the building: a giant armadillo attempting to mate with the dome of the capitol. The governor denounced the painting, claiming that the picture was an obscene slander on the honor of Texas.

"Sounds like fun, but Mexico calls."

We puttered down the freeway past the university; the campus was anchored by the Tower, the million-volume library that was one of Austin's tallest buildings. Ever since Whitman went on his shooting spree, the Tower made a lot of people nervous. In fact, the university had recently closed the Tower to visitors due to a string of suicides—student jumpers who cracked under the pressure of school, or, in at least one case, a fellow with a low draft number decided to go down before being sent to Nam.

Bob drove out of his way to drop us on the south side of town where we could snag a ride easily. Back then, we all helped each other since we were all we had. Too often it was just us, our stoned tribe against the redneck army that occupied all of the state except for Austin. It seemed strange to pass through town without stopping, but we were making good time and wanted to reach the border by dark so we could score a cheap room in Reynosa.

"You see," the foreigner said, "it's so different in my country."

He was a petroleum engineering student at Texas A&I in Kingsville. He pushed his new Mustang to over a hundred miles an hour.

"It looks a lot like here, in some places." He nodded to the blur of brown brush and rocky rises that clouded the windows of the car. "But we don't live like you do."

"Where's that again?" I asked.

"Saudi Arabia."

The Saudi floored the car to a hundred and twenty; the lines on the highway didn't seem to have any spaces between them.

"Better slow her up."

He slowed to ninety.

"How's it so different?" Christi asked. "Back home, I mean."

"You see, we don't drink the beer like the Texans do, and never there would be a pretty woman like you standing on the side of the highway seeking a ride from men. Never would the mullahs allow that."

He took one hand off the wheel and patted Christi's thigh.

"And we don't have the hippies." He shook his head. "You hippies, you are something. You take the drugs and you sleep with anyone."

He glanced at me in the rear view.

"I mean, maybe the three of us could . . . ."

He moved his hand higher on Christi's leg.

"I don't know what they told you about hippies, but if you can't keep your hands on the wheel, pull over and let us out."

The Saudi laughed.

"Here? You want out here?"

We were south of Alice, in the true middle of nowhere: nothing but open highway and scrub desert between us and the Valley.

"Yes, let us out. Now."

"A-okay, mister hippie."

He slammed on the breaks; Christi braced herself against the dash.

"Out. Get out of my car."

I waited until Christi cleared the front seat and stood safely on the shoulder of 281, and then I pushed our packs onto highway and climbed out. The Saudi sped away with screeching tires and a cloud of burning rubber. Christi and I stood on the shoulder of the road, bathing in the heat. There wasn't a car or truck in sight.

As the sun slid across the western sky and the temperature settled down to about 100, we waited, and waited, and waited: nothing but wind and heat.

Christi tucked her hair into her hat.

"If we ever get to Mexico, we're going to take the bus. I've had enough of this fun for a while."

I could only agree.

I didn't like hitching at night, so as darkness shadowed the brush, we jumped a barbed wire fence, walked into a ravine, and settled down. We didn't need the tent since it hadn't rained in about a month and there would be no rain until the next tropical storm curled its moisture off the Gulf of Mexico. Instead of starting a fire, we ate peanut butter and crackers washed down by water and an after dinner joint. We spread out our bags and lay down, counting the stars as they appeared until darkness grew and the stars outnumbered our math.

We were quiet for a long time, lying there, watching the sky. Once in a while we heard a car or truck on the highway.

Finally, Christi turned to face me.

"Don't fall in love. I'll be gone in the fall."

"It may be too late."

The stars continued to multiply above us.

"You'll never know how much it meant to me, that first time. You asked if I had taken any *precautions*, that was the word you used. But I can't stay, can't change my plan. Lack of planning led to my first disaster."

Christi's plan was a good one: transfer to Stanford to improve the odds of getting into med school. We would return from Mexico in August; in September, her father would drive her to California. I planned to stay in school and avoid fighting with my father. In other words, I had no plan.

"Plans change all the time. I could go to California. Cut my hair. Get a job."

Christi was silent; tears shone like stars in her eyes.

The night I met Christi I was running down Guadalupe Street about fifty yards ahead of a cloud of tear gas and maybe a hundred yards in front of the first line of riot-geared police who were swinging night clubs and bashing the heads of anyone who was too slow or too stoned to move. The regular Saturday afternoon antiwar demonstration had evolved into a Yippie street party complete with red flags and a bonfire in the middle of Guadalupe. The cops were content to wait out the party, wait until the hippies smoked enough dope and the Yippies burned enough junk furniture to lose interest and wander home. But before that could happen, some crazy ran down the sidewalk, hammer in hand, smashing storefront windows like he was playing a cymbal. That was too much for the cops. They lowered the visors on their helmets, fired off a volley of gas, and proceeded to march, nightsticks swinging, into the crowd. I passed the university bookstore and Christi opened a door to the stairs leading up to the offices of the *Rag*, Austin's underground paper, and Middle Earth, the drug crisis intervention center.

"Here. In here."

I ducked through the open door and onto the stairs a few yards ahead of the police. Christi locked the door behind me, and we hurried upstairs and stood at the

49

window of the crisis center, frozen as we watched the cops club protester after protester. The pavement turned red and the tear gas wafted over the street and onto the campus.

In the corner of the room, a Middle Earther watched a bum-tripper moan and toss. The Middle Earth staff was famous for talking down the victims of bad LSD or those with weak psychological constitutions—those who should have never experimented with hallucinogens. There were many drug victims among our tribe, a lot of crashes and causalities: kids who got lost when they moved from pot to acid to speed.

"He's okay. Needs a few more hours to come down, is all."

"I'm Kent." I watched out the window as more cops rushed past the building, chasing the protesters north on Guadalupe. "Thanks for saving me."

The next morning, we stood in the early sun waiting for a ride south.

"You know what I liked best about Guatemala?"

"What?"

"I liked that it's not here. It'll be that way in Mexico, too. When we cross that river we're in another country, a country that doesn't own us."

"What exactly were you doing in Guatemala?"

"Well, after the event, I mean, after I delivered the baby girl, I couldn't return to school for the senior prom. Waco is still like a small town. My folks have a 'position.' When I think back, the whole thing was a big stereotype. But I was only sixteen."

The way she said "I was only sixteen" made it sound as if turning nineteen brought a century's worth of wisdom.

"Anyway, Father had one of his doctor buddies arrange

for me to work in a clinic in the highlands. That's where I developed my plan."

Finally, an eighteen-wheeler hauling an empty trailer pulled over. The driver rolled down his window as I walked up.

"Where you going?" He mopped the sweat from his bald head with a rag.

"Mexico."

"Think the girl can ride up back?"

"She'll be okay."

"Then come aboard. I'll going to cross at Reynosa. You'll have to climb down there to go through customs."

I helped Christi scramble over the truck's tires and onto the trailer, and then I handed up our packs and jumped onto the truck bed. The driver gave us a minute to situate ourselves behind the cab window, and we were gone, cutting through the miles of brush country toward the Valley.

The land began to change, to flatten; finally, the scrub and brush surrendered to the Rio Grande delta. Before too long we were passing fields that stretched straight-rowed to the horizon. And in those fields of cabbages and onions the people, the Mexicans, worked, looking like dots on the gridded rows. I had never been to the Valley before, and I couldn't help but wonder what it was like in Mexico, what could make people move north to pick crops in the blazing humidity for a few dollars a day. I remembered what my father said: "When you see how tough it is down there . . . ." Maybe Dad was right: I was only a spoiled kid wasting my time chasing dope and skirts.

Then there was development, some motels, a shopping center, Edinburg, McAllen, and, after a few more miles, Hidalgo, the bridge, and the border crossing.

"Mexico."

The way Christi said the word made it sound magical.

The big truck took us across the bridge, past the U.S. flag. Below, the Rio rolled fast and green with water released from Falcon Lake. The driver pulled into a lane for Mexican customs, and we climbed down from the bed of the eighteen wheeler. I remembered my father's silence as he drove me to the outskirts of Fort Worth. I remembered "Rudolf," the beer-drinking cowboy who gave me my first ride. I remembered his battered pickup truck and the radio blaring out that Johnny Rodriguez song. We had ridden our thumbs to Mexico, ridden away from our parents, our troubles and our separate futures, at least for a while.

Learning the Colors

D allas, Texas 1955

It was a bluebird day—bright sunshine and blue skies and cool temperatures. Soon they were downtown where the big department stores lined the streets and where crowds of people stopped in front of the shop windows to look at the newest clothes. Nancy parked the car, helped Jane out, and deposited a nickel in the parking meter. Then she took her daughter's hand and led the way up the block to the department store entrance. Nancy was proud of her daughter. Jane had her father's blond hair and her mother's blue eyes, and everyone knew that Jane was the brightest five-year-old in the neighborhood. Even the kindergarten teacher was impressed with her; few of the other children could read, and some didn't even know the alphabet, but Jane was able to read and write as well as most second graders.

They stepped through the big, revolving door. The air was filled with wonderful aromas: popcorn and roasted nuts from the candy counter, hamburgers frying on the grill at the rear of the store, and the smell of all those new, never-yet- worn clothes.

"Now follow close. We've got to go upstairs."

They walked through the store and boarded the elevator. Nancy pushed a button and clutched Jane's hand.

The elevator door closed, and then up, up they went. They jerked to a stop, the door slid open, and Jane and her mother stepped out into the ladies' wear department.

Nancy glanced around, looking for a saleswoman, while Jane looked back at the elevator as the door shut all by itself. The department store was an enchanted place full of delights just waiting to be discovered.

A tall, dark haired woman wearing a green dress walked over to Nancy.

"Can I help you?"

"Yes, I came to pick up a dress that was being altered."

"I'll get it for you. What was that name again?"

"Matthews. Nancy Matthews."

The woman went behind her counter, looked through a file, then went back to the fitting rooms for the dress.

Jane spotted yet another wonder of the fantastic department-store world. There were two water fountains standing on either side of the elevator. The fountains were identical, but the signs above the fountains were different. Above the fountain on her left, the sign said WHITE. Above the fountain on Jane's right, the sign said COLORED. Jane had seen a lot of water fountains at her school, but never a water fountain that had colored water. What color would the water be? Would there be a stream of red water, or would the color of the water change from red to blue to green? Jane looked again at the other water fountain, trying to recall if she'd ever seen white water. No, she decided. All the water she had ever seen coming from fountains had been clear, not white, or red, or green, but clear, like air.

The clerk returned with Nancy's dress, a white party outfit.

"That's the one." Nancy smiled, knowing she'd look sexy wearing that dress to the country club.

54

"Would you like to try it on?"

"Yes, I would."

Nancy took the dress from the saleswoman and turned to her daughter who was staring wide-eyed in the direction of the elevator and the water fountains.

"Darling, will you be a big girl and wait right here for Mother?"

"Okay."

"I'll keep my eye on her."

"This will only take a second."

Nancy walked toward the fitting rooms with the dress draped over her arm. The saleswoman smiled at Jane and then returned to her cash register. Jane had to know what color the water would be. She walked over to the fountain that said WHITE, stood on tiptoe, and pushed the button down. There was water all right, but there was nothing special about it. The water was clear, not white. Jane took a long drink. The water tasted like regular water. Why would the sign say WHITE? Jane walked over to the other water fountain, again stood on tiptoe, and again pushed the button. This water was like ordinary water, too, like plain water from any tap.

Then, while Jane was standing tiptoed at the water fountain, a Negro lady and her little boy came over. The woman pushed the elevator button, glanced at Jane, smiled, and waited. The little boy looked and Jane and tugged at his mother's arm. Suddenly the elevator door slid open, and the Negro lady pulled her son into the elevator.

"That one's for us, you know," the little boy said to Jane as the elevator door closed.

Jane wondered what he meant. She had seen Negro people before. Some of them worked in the kitchen at her school, but this was the first time one of them had ever spoken to her. She pushed the fountain button once again, hoping that maybe the colored water was slow in flowing.

"Jane, Jane, come here."

Jane turned and ran to her mother's side.

"What were you doing over there?"

"Only playing." Jane sensed that something was wrong.

"I'm sorry Mrs. Matthews," the clerk said. "I looked away a moment."

"It's all right." Nancy handed the dress to the clerk. "And don't you ever wander off like that again, young lady."

The clerk wrapped the dress and returned it to Nancy. Then Jane and her mother went over to the elevator and waited to go downstairs. The water fountains stood like soldiers on either side of the elevator. Finally, the door opened and Nancy and Jane got in.

"Mother, the colored water isn't working."

"Yes." Nancy struggled to keep her new dress from getting wrinkled. "That's right."

The elevator stopped at the ground floor, and the door opened.

"Come on, darling. Let's get some ice cream."

The Cook's Tale

Ah, thanks friends. A good brew makes good friends, and I can tell you're all fine fellows. I'm glad I stopped here, now, at this inn. I almost passed by, thinking the place looked a little seedy, like the sort Harry Bailey might run. But now I see you are decent fellows here, long of beard and short of tongue, and with the ears to hear me out. Hodge is my name, and I hail from Ware though I've cooked in London for many a year now, and if you buy me another tankard of ale, I'll tell you a tale, a story so lively that its likes have not been heard in this dull pub.

I'm a cook you see, and that's why I went along on the trip in the first place. God knows I didn't go because I longed to kiss some martyr's bones or to say my prayers bent-knee upon a floor of holy stone! I know my craft, and that's a fact. And that's why the tradesmen hired me. They knew I'd feed them well while we were on the road. Not every fellow is willing to do for himself around a stove or a fire, and that's why a cook's for hire. And sharp fellows they were too. Smart enough to leave their women folk at home.

They commissioned me to make their stew, or broil their chicken, or bake a meat pie or two. They paid me well, supplying all the ale I could drink. Believe me, I put a dent in their fat purses, but I knew they had the capital and the revenue.

Yes, those boys were okay. But the others, some twenty or so, what a row they caused! Always at each other's throats. All in all, I thought they were a sorry lot. I'll tell you a thing or two about that crew, and I'll finish my tale as well, the one the poet cut short. Of course, he had to humor all the religious folk who rode along. It was like traveling with a church. I'll say this though, some of those church people weren't so saintly.

Why, there was a Monk who dressed in mink. His hands were soft and pink. He wasn't one to labor and toil as he'd been taught. He would have been a good match for the Prioress—the only things she loved were her little dogs. Fed them meat and bread she did, and told a story as cold as her heart, a tale of slit throats and Jews hung from carts. *Amor vincit omnia*—love conquers all—was her motto, but that was not the moral of her story. And that Summoner, by Saint Thomas! What an ugly fart he was with his talk of Hell and twenty thousand friars crawling up the Devil's arse! But some of the others were fakers, too. The Physician had a taste for gold, but nothing he could do would keep a body from growing old. And that Wife from Bath—pray you never cross her path. Seems she killed her husbands every one. Why, she was searching for her next victim when our trip begun.

Then there was Sir Knight. What a braggart. To have fought in all the battles that he told, well, he'd have to be a hundred years old! And the Squire who rode with him, what a whimp. He was always talking love and piping on his lute. I made him out to be a fruit. And as I recall, the Squire and the Pardoner were always falling behind the rest—what they were up to I can only guess.

The Yeoman seemed to be a good sort, though, as did the Clerk from Oxford. But of the church folk, only the Parson was worth a damn, and he bored us to death with his sermon. Seven deadly sins my arse! But worst of all was the Host, old Bailey, who led us to every dirty inn on the way and made us pay his friends who owned these dens. Harry Bailey was his name, and he did all right, I'd say, taking kickbacks from his fellow crooks all the way.

That Bailey—I'll settle with him yet—knock him on the chin some dark night when he steps out back the Tabard to piss in his customer's brew. He had great fun at my expense: that little sore upon my shin. You'd think a bruise was such a sin. And truth be told, that ulcer upon my knee was nothing more than a burn I got while lifting a pot of peas.

With this Bailey rode his pal, the Manciple. He knew a hundred ways to short a lawyer. Called me a swine, he did, and pushed me from my horse—made out like I was drunk. Why, I only drank the wine he offered to ease the pain in my sore rump. Old Bailey was right to warn him that I'd take revenge. I knew about that crooked pair even then. To top it all, they wouldn't let me finish my tale. That poet fellow cut my story out and pictured me to be a drunken lout!

But say, my tankard's dry again, and for another pint I'll finish the tale I tried to tell those folk. Ah, thanks mate. You know, telling stories is a great cause of dry throat. Now hear my tale of love and woe. For when it comes to matters of love and money, even a friend can be a foe.

It's the story of Revelling Peterkin—that's what folk called him because he passed his time in drink and sin. Peterkin was slight of build and brown and crafty as a Moor. He took an apprenticeship to learn the grocery business, but his real trade was playing dice. He played in secret games or on streets where such is done, and when he won, he won. But when he lost, he lost, and he'd pick the shop's till to pay the cost. When his master found him out, the minstrels played and led the way as Peterkin was jailed. Finally his pal, Jim, paid the bail.

Jim was a good-looking fellow, thin and rakish with dull blue eyes and greasy blond hair that fell about his shoulders. They called him "Sipping Jim" because he worked in a wine house stacking kegs. He had mastered the art of tapping a cask with a straw. The owners never missed the drinks he'd draw. After a few drinks, Jim would begin to swagger and play with the little dagger that he always carried tucked under his belt.

Like his pal Peterkin, Jim was a gambler. They were as much partners as pals. You know, there's never a thief but has a buddy to help him milk a sucker. So it was with Peterkin and Jim. They were a team that conned many a bearded merchant out of his profits in crooked games of cards or dice. When Peterkin was sprung from jail, Jim kindly invited his pal to stay with him. So Peterkin sent his bundle and his bed to Jim's place where he planned to live until his luck changed.

Now just as Peterkin had relied on the till at the shop to cover his gambling losses, Jim had a sort of till he could count on, too. He had a cute little girl. She called herself Sue. She was fair of face but dark of eye and hair, with a tight little figure—nice little breasts and all the rest. Her body was as slender as any weasel's and as soft and tender. Sue had a lecherous eye, and she had plucked her eyebrows into bows. And there was no fault with her nose. If flaw be found, it can be said that Sue was a bit gap-toothed, but that was suitable considering her lusty nature. To save her good repute, she kept a job at a store. But plying flesh was her real trade. She made her living by getting laid. In a word, she was a whore, and a good one too. Sue made many a score with tradesmen and churchmen. Why I wouldn't doubt that the Monk or Friar who rode with us had tried her favors out.

Jim and Sue had a little place outside the city gate—a one-room cottage with a roof of crumbling thatch. Peterkin settled in this little home, tossing his pallet on the floor before the fire and leaving Jim and Sue the bed that was hidden behind curtains in a corner of the room. One morning, Jim left for work, leaving Peterkin to sleep it off in front of the hearth. Now Peterkin woke thinking that he might burst, so he went outside and pissed against the cottage wall. Then he went back into the house and crawled in bed with Sue.

Sue had worked till late the night before, screwing some Reeve out of his money—and before she had fully come to, Peterkin was in her and had done his do. The scene was repeated the very next day. Indeed, whenever Jim's work kept him away, Peterkin and Sue were sure to play.

Now Sue was a good girl at heart, and she would take Peterkin in her arms and stroke him, saying "You're a fine one for sure. But still, you'll have to pay to share my bed."

Sue had her professional standards, and Peterkin, being broke and out of work, told her to start a tab. His luck would change someday and then he would pay her for all her lays.

But sure as I'm Hodge the cook from Ware, you're all wise fellows, and so you know that a tale like this has but one way to go. Jim returned home early one afternoon and caught the lovers in full action. He could clearly see that Peterkin was getting satisfaction.

"So this is how you repay a pal."

Jim drew his dagger from his belt. Caught by surprise, Peterkin jumped off of Sue and hid behind the bed.

"Go easy there," he said. "I've told Sue I'll pay what's

61

due."

Jim glanced at his girl. She pulled the blanket around herself and nodded that it was true.

"You see!"

Peterkin trembled. He was afraid that he might be dead if he couldn't change the thought in Jim's head.

"If that's the case then where's the pay?   Besides, it's low of a friend to screw a buddy's girl this way."

Jim waved his dagger through the air. Peterkin he had no intent to spare.

"We're partners and pals," Peterkin begged. "I promise that someday I'll pay."

"Settle up now or I'll have my pound of flesh starting with what you've been sharing with Sue."

At this Peterkin fainted to the floor. Jim stepped forward. The blade glittered in the light that streamed in through the open door.

"No, wait," begged Sue. "Let's make a sport of this. You're both gaming men. Let's wager and see who'll win."

"There's no gamble here," Jim said.

But still, he stepped back and let the dagger in his hand go slack.

Sue glanced at Peterkin who huddled on the floor.

"Listen, I say we let a roll of the dice decide our actions. If Peterkin wins, the score is settled, and he'll owe nothing for the favors he's enjoyed. If the dice roll your way," she said to Jim, "then you will win."

Jim snorted and said, "What have I to gain?"

"Why, if fortune smiles on you, you'll have every right to do what you will with Peterkin."

"I'll have my way, and I need no dice to say it's so."

Jim stepped forward and waved the blade through the air. Sue fell back against the wall, and Peterkin swooned again, falling flat before the pair.

Jim knelt and placed the point of the dagger against Peterkin's naked shoulder. A trickle of blood ran down Peterkin's arm and pooled on the floor.

"The law will deal harshly with you if you kill him in this manner," Sue said. "But if you gamble with him and win, then no officer can deny you what you've won by right."

Jim pressed the point of the blade a bit deeper. Peterkin whimpered. The pool of red spread and Peterkin grew weaker.

"And if I win this bet," Jim said to Sue, "you'll be my witness when the sheriff comes to ask what passed?"

"I promise to speak the truth, but you must give Peterkin a chance."

Jim recalled his past troubles with the sheriff, withdrew the point of the knife from Peterkin's shoulder, and stood up. He wiped the blade clean on his boot but didn't return the dagger to its sheath.

"All right. We'll have a game and let Chance decide whether or not this cheating Peterkin can keep his hide. We'll let a single throw of the dice speak for Fate, but I'll not roll this crock's dice. We'll throw mine."

Jim cleared the top of the dinner table with one sweep of his knife. Then he took a pair of dice from his pocket, rolled them in his palm, and tossed them on the table. One came up six, the other came up five.

"Eleven."

Jim licked his thumb and moistened the edge of his blade. Sue looked at Peterkin and frowned.

Peterkin moved like a man in shock. He hobbled up to the table with a blanket wrapped around him like a smock. He picked up the dice, stared at them a moment, then tossed them onto the table.

A pair of sixes! What luck!

"Damn you!" Jim planted the blade into the tabletop. "The Wheel has turned. The gaming gods have spoken. My promise to you will not be broken."

Jim gave Sue a cold look. Then he turned and stormed out of the cottage.

Peterkin collapsed into a chair. Sue ran to him and bandaged his wounded shoulder.

"That was genius on your part," Peterkin said. "But how did you know that I would win?"

"But of course I didn't know."

They laughed and fell back into bed, meaning to finish the job they started before Jim discovered them.

Well, thanks friends. I hope you've enjoyed my story, a cook's tale. But listen well to what old Hodge the Cook from Ware says about Simpkin, the Miller. Simpkin's story had a moral too, the same as mine: guests who stay the night are a danger. A man can't be too careful when he brings another into his private things, especially if those things are fair of face, fine of form, and weasel-soft like Sue. That's my story brothers, and I swear it's true. Now I hope someone will buy me another brew.

The Road to Roma

I

J ill McDaniel slowed her car to a crawl when she spotted the house where the television doctor lived. It was a large two-story built of red brick and tucked away behind a long lawn shaded by tall pecan trees. She pulled into the drive, brushed her short brown hair, and straightened her suit jacket. Then she got out of the car and surveyed the quiet street once again. Highland Park was an island, a "bubble" of wealth surrounded by the disaster that was Dallas.

She took her memo pad out of her purse and reviewed the notes she made concerning Dr. William Jackson. Jill discovered a lot about Dr. Jackson simply by making a few phone calls. Jackson built a family practice in Dallas before he started doing television work. His first shows were public service medical bulletins aired as late night features on a local station. Later, Dr. Jackson hosted a thirty-minute question and answer program on medical problems. The program was so successful that the station made it a weekly show. Then the series was syndicated, and the reruns were broadcast statewide. From Amarillo to Brownsville, from Beaumont to El Paso, Texas stations aired *Dr. Bill's Medicine Show*. In only a few years, William

Jackson had gone from family physician to celebrity. Lately, he had become active in conservative political circles.

Jill walked across the lawn of close-cut Bermuda grass and guessed that the girl was a runaway. Kids who lived in the nicer neighborhoods were always likely to feel the need to escape.

The door opened before Jill could raise her finger to the bell.

"Miss McDaniel?"

The woman who greeted Jill was certainly not a domestic; a trim blonde about thirty years old, she wore a revealing sun dress and had an expression on her face that proclaimed her power and comfort.

"Yes, that's me."

The woman gave Jill a quick smile and motioned for her to enter the hallway.

"This way please."

She led Jill down the hall, past a dining room that had white carpeting, white walls, and white furniture, and into the doctor's study. The room was large and bright with windows that faced the patio and swimming pool. The pool looked cool and inviting, a refuge from the hot summer afternoon. Bookcases lined the walls of Jackson's office, and the polished wood floor gleamed in the sunlight that streamed in through the windows. Dr. Jackson's desk occupied one corner of the office. It was a black metal desk so long and sleek that it reminded Jill of an operating table.

"Make yourself comfortable."

"Thanks."

Jill took a seat in one of the leather chairs that faced the desk.

"Dr. Jackson will be with you shortly. Can I get you anything?"

"Coffee would be nice."

When the woman left the room, Jill got up from her chair and began snooping around the doctor's study. Unfortunately, Dr. Jackson was a neat man. The only thing on the desk was that morning's newspaper. *The Dallas Morning Snooze*, the locals called it. The headline declared that the Greeks and Turks were about to go to war over Cyprus. It seemed that 1974 was going to be a troubled year.

Jill surveyed the titles in the doctor's library. There were plenty of medical texts and an entire shelf of *National Geographic* magazines. Nothing anyone would want to steal, Jill thought as she thumbed through a text concerned with the treatment of alcoholism.

She put the book back on the shelf and turned toward the door as Dr. Jackson came into the room. What surprised Jill most about Jackson was his size. Jill had seen the doctor's television program many times, and the man looked much taller on the TV than he did in person. But even though he wasn't tall, he had a tight, wide-shouldered body that looked good in a blue blazer and charcoal slacks and proved that he took his exercise seriously. Jill figured him to be fifty something, and Dr. Jackson would have looked younger if his hair had not gone completely gray.

"I'm so glad you decided to discuss this matter with me in person," Dr. Jackson said.

He shook Jill's hand and led her back to her chair before he sat down behind his desk.

"I had to come to Dallas anyway. You want me to find your missing daughter, right?"

"Well, it's a little more involved than that. Actually, I know where my daughter is."

There was a knock on the door and lady in the summer dress came in with a tray of coffee and snack cakes. She sat the tray on the doctor's desk and quietly turned and left the room, closing the door behind her.

"How do you like yours?"

"Black, please."

Dr. Jackson poured them each a cup of coffee, and Jill helped herself to one of the snack cakes.

"So your daughter's not a runaway?"

"No," Dr. Jackson said. "It's much worse than that." He took a sip of coffee. "She's a student at the University of Texas."

"I see."

"You know how things are down at the University. I mean Austin was always a party town, but they've let it go too far."

"Humm, good cake."

"They are good, aren't they? Betsy makes a fresh batch every week."

"Betsy? Your wife?"

"Betsy's my friend. Actually, one reason there's a problem with my daughter is because my wife and I divorced last year. It was quite a battle, and Pam, that's my daughter, well, she took the break up pretty hard."

Dr. Jackson watched Jill as she finished eating the snack cake.

"If you know where your daughter is, what exactly do you want me to do?"

"You've seen my television program?"

"Who hasn't?"

"*Dr. Bill's Medicine Show* has brought me a lot of exposure. So much exposure that we're planning to open a chain of hospitals offering treatment for those involved in substance abuse, drugs, in other words. We're calling the hospitals the Smarter Vista Clinics."

"Good name."

"I'm also considering a run for office on an anti-drug platform. Drugs, the abuse of drugs and liquor, that is the number one threat facing our state. It's a threat that we can only fight with tough laws and tough rehab programs."

It was a line he planned to use in his campaign.

"But before I attempt a run for office, even before I can open my substance abuse clinics, I need to know if my daughter might become an embarrassment to me."

"I understand," Jill said. "You want me to find out if your little girl has gotten herself into any difficult situations down in wicked Austin town."

Doctor Jackson sipped at his coffee, but he didn't smile.

"I hardly expect her to be a saint, you know. There's too much of her mother in her for that. But if there's trouble, I want to know now."

"Surveillance isn't really my specialty. Most of the time I do research. You know, title checks, insurance reports, that sort of thing."

"I was told that you are one of the best investigators in Austin."

"Oh, really?" Jill felt the flush of a blush. "You say your divorce was difficult. Where is your former wife now?"

"Busy drinking up all the rum in the Caribbean. Her constant boozing drove a wedge between us. Of course, Pam thinks that I drove her mother to drink." Dr. Jackson looked away for a moment. "Pam's a very confused young woman."

Dr. Jackson unlocked the drawer of his desk, removed a photograph, and handed the picture to Jill.

"That's Pam at her high school graduation four years ago."

Jill looked at the photo of the pretty blonde dressed in black academic robes.

"She's lovely."

"Yes, she is. Looks like her mother."

"Any reason to suspect that she's involved with trouble?"

"No, nothing I know of. But nothing is the trouble. I never hear from her. I've never even seen the house she lives in. When I try to arrange a visit, she puts me off. Since her mother and I divorced, the only thing that's passed between Pam and me is money—tuition and expenses for college."

"Since you've brought the subject up, this type of case, simple as it is, can cost a substantial amount."

Dr. Jackson took another sip of coffee and then looked at Jill. She could feel his eyes touching her.

"Miss McDaniel. I do my homework. I didn't expect that your services would come cheaply. But I was assured that you would be discrete."

Jill put the photograph of Pam in her purse.

"No need to worry. The dirt I dig up will be our dirt, no one else's."

Rango—his real name was Ralph, but he had taken to calling himself *Rango* that year—was decked out in high red- neck fashion when he showed up at Chris' Discount Liquor. He had squeezed himself into a pair of faded Levis and managed to button half of the mother-of-pearl snaps on his yellow cowboy shirt. His embossed two-tone boots were made of snake skin, and he wore a wide-brimmed felt hat with a little red feather in the band. He walked up to the counter and ordered a case of Lone Star longnecks and two bottles of Blue Nun wine.

The clerk working the counter gave Rango a wink.

"Got a date tonight, don't you?"

"Now, Gary, why would you think that?"

"Because all the years I've known you I never seen you

drink anything except beer or whiskey. I sure never knew you to be a wine sipper."

Gary started toward the store's walk-in cooler. He was young, only twenty-three, but he wasn't soft—months of lifting cases of wine and unloading liquor trucks had made him tough enough. He carried the case of beer out to Rango's pickup truck, and the young men stood in the back corner of the parking lot, watching the cars stream south on Lamar. The daily migration of office workers fleeing downtown Austin for the suburbs was well underway. Gary glanced at his watch and decided that Chris, the boss, wouldn't miss him for a few minutes.

"I want you to come to a party. You need to meet Jim-bo."

"I don't want anything to do with that guy," Gary said.

"Oh, come on. It's only a party."

"I'll talk to Pam about it."

Rango smiled and climbed into his truck while Gary shuffled back into the liquor store.

Chris was waiting at the counter when he came back inside. Chris was a fat little Greek who had been in the States for twenty-five years. He lived for the shipments of cheese and black olives that arrived at the store from Greece, and he read every scrap of news he could find about the trouble on Cyprus. He was a soft-hearted guy who liked everyone except the Turks, and even though Gary sometimes made fun of him because all Chris ever did was work, the work had paid off. Chris had arrived in the States without a dime; now he owned four liquor stores in Austin and had three sons who managed his other locations.

When Gary walked over to the counter, Chris put down the *Austin American-Statesman*.

"Who is that guy?"

"That fellow? That was Ralph, my old friend. He calls himself Rango now, but you see him in here every week."

"Something about that boy. I don't go for those clothes."

"Ah, he's a drugstore cowboy who keeps busy chasing skirts, is all."

Chris shook his head and went back to reading about the Greeks and the Turks and what was happening half a world away while Gary spent the afternoon dusting wine bottles, stocking the cooler, and day dreaming about Pam.

Late that evening, Pam stood naked in front of the mirror and brushed her blonde hair while Gary lay on the bed and read a *National Geographic* article on white-water canoeing in Costa Rica.

Pam had an Irish nose, and her eyes sometimes seemed to vacillate between green and brown. One thing was for sure; Pam was a looker. Rango had once called her "an instant hard on," and Gary suspected that Rango hit on Pam when he wasn't around. Rango's sense of ethics, especially when it came to women, wasn't very well developed.

Although she didn't spend too much time in class—in fact, she spent more hours working as a cashier at the Dobie Mall parking garage than she spent in school—Pam was big on education because her father sent her money as long as she stayed in college. He was a Dallas doctor—Pam was a Hockaday girl—and he had even given her a new Ford Mustang for her birthday. Pam was well known among the departmental secretaries at the University of Texas as the student most likely to set a record for changing majors. Pam tried nursing when she wanted to help the sick, pre-law when she believed that lawyers served justice, education when she read Freire's *Pedagogy of the Oppressed*, and psychology when she felt sorry for herself. About the only major she hadn't tried was English; even Pam couldn't figure out how getting an English degree could help anything.

"I guess it wouldn't hurt to go." She watched herself in the mirror as she talked. "After all, it's just a party."

"I don't think we should get mixed up with that bunch. It's a tough crowd. But we can go if you really want."

Pam turned away from the mirror and lay down on the bed next to Gary. She gave him a long, slow kiss, and he ran his hands over her breasts.

"Jesus, you're so soft."

"Come on, honey."

She got up, went into the bathroom, turned on the bath water, and stepped into the tub. As the tub filled with water, Gary knelt and started soaping Pam's back and sponging her legs. Then he climbed into the bath, and in a minute he was inside her, warm and safe from the world as the water sloshed out of the tub and onto the floor.

Jill leaned back in the seat of her Cougar and emptied the remainder of her thermos into a coffee cup. She was parked on a quiet Austin street in a neighborhood called the Avenues, a mile or so north of the university campus. It was a warm September evening, and the only activity on the street was at the shotgun duplex at the end of the corner.

Jill sipped her coffee and wrote in the notebook she had reserved for the Pam Jackson case. So far, Jill hadn't come up with much. Okay, so the girl was living with some guy, Jill thought. At least the fellow was clean-cut, not long haired and shabby like most the boys around the campus.

Jill closed the notebook, put the binoculars down on the seat, and took another sip of coffee. Then she started her car and headed back to her apartment.

That Saturday, Pam and Gary drove to Rango's house in Pam's Mustang. The grass needed mowing because Rango never cut his yard; he claimed that he wanted to keep things organic. Gary knocked on the door and waited. It always took Rango a long time to unlock his house. Rango's place was a four-bedroom ranch-style on the northeast fringe of Austin's city limits. The house hadn't been painted in years, but it had a comfortable look to it because of the cluster of old pecan trees that shaded the front porch.

"Hey, come on in."

Rango had a towel wrapped around his waist, his curly red hair was still wet from a shower, and there was a spot of shaving lather on his chin. He held the door open for Pam and Gary, and they followed him through the den and into the kitchen.

"You guys got here faster than I planned. Give me a minute and I'll be with you."

Rango went back into the bathroom, and Pam and Gary sat down at the kitchen table. Rango's kitchen was as well kept as his yard. Dishes were stacked in the sink, and leftover food and empty beer bottles covered the counters.

"He should hire a maid," Pam said. "I don't know how he stands it."

She was obsessed with neatness, and even though the shotgun apartment she shared with Gary was small, she always kept it clean and tidy.

Pam and Gary met in a government class called "The Politics of Peace." As the days slid away and the professor spent the class time explaining how positive thinking could overcome the world's political and economic problems, Gary and Pam did some thinking about each other. Before long, they had moved in together.

Everything had worked out fine until Gary discovered that Pam had been sleeping with the lead singer of a rock band called Leaky Seals. Gary had moved out for nearly a month then, but at last Pam broke up with the singer and begged Gary to come home. That was when Gary realized that he couldn't say no to Pam Jackson.

Rango came into the room and sat down at the kitchen table. He wore pressed jeans and a white cowboy shirt that made him look like one of those guys who rushed out onto the football field anytime Texas scored a touchdown.

"Believe me, amigos. This will be a great party."

For the millionth time Gary wondered why Rango insisted upon calling everybody amigo. It bothered Gary because he really was Rango's friend. Gary and Rango had known each other almost all of their lives. They grew up together in McAllen and the Rio Grande Valley. They played on the same Little League team, went to same summer camp, and were bored by the same teachers at school. Their fathers were hunting buddies, and they always took the boys along when they went down to Mexico to shoot white-wing doves.

The boys had always been friends, but the wreck that killed their parents had made them like brothers. That was when Rango and Gary were seniors in high school. Their parents were down in Ciudad Victoria for a weekend fishing trip. From what the boys could learn from the Mexican police, a drunk driver doing an estimated ninety miles per hour plowed into their car on a straight stretch of road south of the border. There wasn't much left to bury when the bodies finally cleared customs.

Pam leaned back in her chair, brushed her long blonde hair over her shoulders, and lit a cigarette. Gary thought Pam looked a lot like Faye Dunaway. Rango got up, fetched a round of beers, and led Gary and Pam out into the backyard where they watched as he inspected his untended garden. Rango pulled up a fistful of weeds and picked a lone tomato off a vine that had gone brown.

"Sure going to miss these tomatoes. The store bought ones taste like chemicals to me."

Rango bit into the overripe fruit, dribbling juice down his chin. He used the sleeve of his shirt for a napkin.

"We better get going," Rango said at last. "Party will be over by the time we get there."

The early fall weather was perfect for a barbecue in the country—warm but not hot. As Pam, Gary, and Rango drove though Austin, the afternoon seemed to bounce with sunshine and blue sky. They stopped at Chris' store for a six- pack and caught Chris at lunch. He had recently received a shipment of cheese and black olives, and he insisted that everyone sample some food from the old country.

"These are the real black olives." Chris handed Pam a slice of cheese and three large olives neatly folded into a paper cocktail napkin. "Not like the ones they import from Spain."

Pam took a taste.

"They are different. Very good."

"I have them shipped to me each month. Five gallons at a time."

They thanked Chris for the treat and went out to the car. A new Cougar convertible was parked next to their Mustang, and Rango whistled under his breath at the brunette behind the wheel.

"Man, look at her." Rango settled himself into the back seat of the Mustang. "I'd like to get her top down."

"When did you start taking such an interest in cars?"

"You're a clever fellow, amigo," Rango said.

Pam eyed the brunette as the woman got out of the Cougar and went into the liquor store.

"I don't know how you could get the hots for some thirty-year old when I'm around." Pam started up the car. "If that old lady ever knew what to do, she's probably forgotten it by now."

Pam drove west on 71, and before long they were clear of the last stretch of suburb and were speeding up and down the low hills that were green with scrub cedar. They slowed down for the town of Bee Cave and finally turned off on a farm road that brought them, after a few minutes of dusty driving, to the gate of Jimbo's ranch.

A young cowboy who was built big enough to have played tackle for any west Texas high school checked Rango's invitation, tipped his black Stetson to Pam, and swung the gate open.

The dust from Pam's car hadn't had time to settle when Jill McDaniel pulled up in front of the gate and shifted her Cougar into park. She took off her sunglasses and brushed back her hair as the guard approached.

"Can I help you ma'am?"

"Please." Jill took a crumpled road map from the dashboard. "I'm afraid I'm completely lost. I was headed for Spicewood, trying to cut though on the back roads, and now I'm all confused."

"Yes, ma'am." The big cowboy eyed Jill cautiously. "I would say you are lost."

He showed Jill the right road on her map, and she thanked him, turned her car around, and sped off.

Jimbo's place wasn't large enough by Texas standards to qualify as a working ranch, but it was about the right size to keep as a hobby. The house was built of native limestone, and it had a wide, screened-in porch across the front and a patio off the back. There were twenty or so people on the porch, drinks in hand, and one of them, a tall, dark-haired fellow in blue jeans and a white cowboy shirt, just the sort that Rango wore, waved to Rango when Pam pulled the car into the yard.

"That's Jimbo."

"He doesn't look too tough to me," Gary said.

Rango laughed as they got out of the car.

"He might not look tough, but I wouldn't want to tangle with him. One time I saw him cut off a man's fingers."

"All of them?"

"No, only the ones on the left hand."

"Why did he do that?"

"The fellow was a thief."

"God," Pam said. "I feel a little sick."

"Hey, amigo," Jimbo called to Rango. "How's it going? These must be your buddies."

Jimbo had thick black hair and deep, dark brown eyes that made him look younger than his forty years. He stood about six-two in his cowboy boots and weighed about one-ninety. Jimbo was in good shape; he had played some ball himself in his younger days.

"That's right. This here is Pam, and this is my good friend Gary."

"Pleased to know you." Jimbo shook Pam's hand first and then Gary's. "Sure am glad that you could make it out here today. How about a drink?"

They followed Jimbo through his house, heading for the bar that was set up in the back yard. The interior of Jimbo's place was nothing like the ranch style, stone exterior. The furniture was all modern, a utilitarian style with low metal tables and polished rosewood chairs. The kitchen had glass- fronted cabinets and stainless steel counters. A group of people sat at the kitchen table, scooping cocaine out of a fishbowl with tiny silver spoons.

There were more than a hundred people scattered down the softly sloping backyard. The yard was bordered on its far end by a stream, and young men and women lay naked on the manicured bank, taking in the hot afternoon. A few had even ventured into the creek and were skinny-dipping and splashing in the clear water.

A young Mexican manned the bar, and two waiters dressed in identical white uniforms made the rounds through the crowd with trays of drinks and snacks. Gary asked for a Weller and water, Rango wanted a beer, and Pam ordered a gin and tonic. Jimbo drank iced tea.

"Let's take a walk," Jimbo said to Gary.

They went across the yard, through a wooden gate, and into the pasture that paralleled Jimbo's ranch. One side of the field was bordered by a line of low oaks, the other sides by the stream and Jimbo's fenced-off yard. An unpainted cattle shed rusted away at the foot of the grove of oak trees.

"You've known Rango a long time, haven't you?" Jimbo finally asked.

"Yeah. We go back a long way. I even remember when his name was Ralph."

"He told me about your folks and all."

Gary was surprised that Rango had told Jimbo about the wreck. It was something Rango rarely talked about. They walked along the fence line, heading toward the stream. Jimbo looked at the people who were skinny-dipping.

"Water looks good."

"So do the naked girls," Jimbo added.

They stopped walking long enough for Jimbo to light a cigarette.

"What I've got to decide," Jimbo went on, "is what kind of smarts you have."

Gary took a sip of his drink and wondered what Jimbo was leading to.

"You see, brains count a lot in my business. What did Rango tell you about me?"

"He hasn't really said much about you," Gary lied.

"See, that's what I like about Rango. He knows how to keep his mouth shut."

Jimbo smoked his cigarette and stared off at the people sunbathing on the banks of his stream.

"Rango says that you can be trusted. Trust is a valuable commodity in our business, even more valuable than brains. Why don't you work with me? You could kind of be Rango's helper. There's plenty of money in it."

Gary looked toward the creek, and he thought that he saw a flash of reflection from something up on the bluff above the stream. Whatever it was, it didn't flash again.

"Look here. I don't know what Rango told you. But I'm not the guy you want."

"Okay." Jimbo gave Gary a hard look. "I can respect that. I appreciate you being straight with me. But think on it a while. Tell Rango to bring you back out next week. We'll talk more then."

Gary said nothing. They turned and started walking up the fence line.

"You like bird hunting?" Jimbo opened the wooden gate for Gary.

"Sure. Who doesn't?"

"Good. Then let's liven up this party some."

Jill parked the Cougar at the side of the road and took a pair of binoculars and her camera from the trunk before climbing over a barbed wire fence and heading off across the cedar-covered hills. She hiked more than a mile when she found herself on a bluff overlooking a creek and the ranch that she suspected Pam was visiting.

"This has got to be the place," Jill said to herself when she saw the crowd of people on the lawn and noticed the skinny-dippers swimming in the stream below.

She put down her camera bag and focused the binoculars on the party below. Before long she had spotted Pam and Rango standing in the backyard with the other guests. Across the fence Jill saw Pam's boyfriend talking with an older man that she had not seen before. Jill put down the binoculars, took her camera out of its case, and snapped on the telephoto lens. She took a shot of Pam and Rango then clicked off several photos of Gary and Jimbo. She was about to take another picture of Jimbo when she noticed the Mexican servants as they came out of the ranch house carrying shotguns and boxes. She zoomed in one the boxes and saw that they were actually bird cages.

"Well, well. Little Pammie has gone and hooked herself up with a real sportsman here."

Jill packed up the camera, watched the proceedings through her binoculars for a while, then started back to her car before the first boom of the shotguns echoed over the hills.

Gary fired and another bird dropped to the ground. Most of the people at the party had gathered in the pasture across from Jimbo's lawn and were watching as Jimbo, Rango, and Gary shot bird after bird after bird as soon as the Mexicans released them from their cages. Only the very fastest birds escaped the deadly fire. After thirty minutes, a hundred dead pigeons lay scattered across the pasture.

"You fellows are regular hot shots," Jimbo declared as Rango dropped the last bird.

Gary handed his empty shotgun to one of the Mexicans.

"We used to do a lot of dove hunting with our folks."

The servants took the other shotguns and begin gathering the dead pigeons from the field.

"What will they do with the birds?" Pam asked.

"The help will eat well tonight," Jimbo smiled. "Pigeon tacos, you know."

"I don't know what more you expect me to do," Jill said.

She spoke loudly so that Dr. Jackson could hear her despite the poor phone connection. For thirty minutes she had discussed the report she mailed to the doctor, carefully explaining again and again that Pam was living with a young man who wasn't a college student.

"But you don't understand. I've got other projects."

She looked out the window of her apartment at Town Lake. The wind was whipping white-caps across the water, and the gray sky looked like it might storm. Jill wished she could convince Jackson to drop the case; she hated to talk on the phone during thunderstorms.

"Listen, I'm keeping you on full retainer," Jackson told her. "Whenever you get the chance, look in on Pam for me. It'll ease my mind, and you can be certain I'll make it worth your time."

A bright flash of lightening lit the sky to the west, and a peal of thunder soon followed.

"So long as you're willing to pay, I guess I can keep tabs on her."

"You don't know how much that means to me. If something new develops, call me immediately."

"Okay. If that's what you want, okay."

Ever since Jill called him at his office, Bob Maran had been jittery. Sitting at a corner table in Les Amis Restaurant and waiting for Jill to come through the door, he was more nervous than he had been years ago when he and Jill were both students at UT and he finally worked up the courage to ask her for a date. He still remembered that date. They went to the campus theater to see the student actors perform *Romeo and Juliet*. Now, looking back, it seemed to Bob that the play set the tone for their own romance. Like Romeo and Juliet, they were too young to know what was happening to them.

Jill walked into the restaurant, spotted him easily, smiled, and came over to his table. As he got up and greeted her with a hug, Bob thought that being in her thirties hadn't hurt Jill at all. She was more beautiful than ever, even though she was wearing her hair a bit shorter than when he knew her in college.

"Well. At least you haven't gotten fat."

"It's great to see you, too," Bob said.

"I thought it would be fun to check in on you. After all, it's been years."

"How about something to drink."

"A beer would be nice."

Bob ordered beers and they sat quietly and looked each other over until the waitress returned with the drinks.

"Funny. I thought you would be wearing your uniform."

Bob was dressed in a checkered cowboy shirt, blue jeans, and lizard-skin boots.

"Actually, I don't wear my uniform unless I've got a warrant to serve. But I do require my deputies to wear uniforms whenever they're on duty."

"How do you like being a county constable? I never dreamed you would end up being a politician."

Bob smiled and leaned back in his chair.

"I like to think of myself as a peace officer rather than a politician."

"Still, you did run for office and get elected. You must be a least part politician."

"You can thank all the college kids for my election. My opponent was a fellow about as old as the dome on the capitol building. I won on the youth vote. In fact, I'm the youngest constable in Travis County."

"I'm not too surprised. I always knew you'd turn out okay."

"Speaking of surprises, I heard that you're a private investigator. How did that happen?"

"After college I worked for a summer in my dad's law firm as a office assistant. I was thinking of going to law school, and I wanted to get an inside look at a lawyer's world. Anyway, that's where I met some professional investigators, and I thought they had a lot more fun than the attorneys. But I'm thinking of quitting and going for the law degree after all. I'm getting too old for private eye stuff. The hours are terrible."

"You'll make a fine attorney. Hell, I always knew you could be whatever you wanted."

"Someone told me you were in Houston."

"Yeah, I worked with the Houston police for five years before moving back to Austin."

Jill took a sip of her beer and gave Bob a long look.

"I hate to admit it, but I'd really lost track of you until I read in the paper last year that you were running for constable. I meant to call you then, but I never worked up the nerve. I wasn't all that certain that you'd want to hear from me."

Bob gave her a mock frown.

"You know better than that. I'd always be happy to hear from my favorite old girl friend."

"Fill me in on what you've been doing."

Bob sipped on his beer.

"Where should I begin?"

"Start with when you quit college. That's the last time

I saw you."

"Let's see. I worked in my dad's store for a while. Then I joined the Army to keep from getting drafted. They made me an M.P. at Fort Hood. I guess they did that because I had been criminology major. Anyway, I did my time in the service and decided to stay in law enforcement. I took a job in Houston. Then I came back to Austin."

Bob took another sip of his beer.

"You look really great you know. Even better than when we were in school."

Jill smiled and felt the color flood her face.

"Did you ever get married?" she asked.

"Yeah. Biggest mistake I ever made. It lasted six whole months. She couldn't take being a cop's wife."

"Any kids?"

"Nope."

"Well, that's a break. Seems like everybody I know these days divorces right after they have a couple of babies."

"Did you ever get hitched?"

Jill shook her head.

"I had a couple of close calls, but I'm still on my own."

Bob smiled. "I'm glad you called me."

"I really wanted to see you, but I was also sort of hoping you might be able to do me a little favor."

"Please don't tell me this is a business meeting."

"Well, only half business. Let me tell you about my case."

The next morning Bob got out of bed, put on his shirt, and pulled open the curtain that covered the picture window in Jill's bedroom. Jill turned in the bed and looked at Bob as he pulled on his jeans and buckled his belt.

"Plug in the coffee maker. It's all set to go."

"You've got a great view here."

Bob looked out the window onto Town Lake and the Austin skyline. Then he went into the kitchen and started coffee while Jill got out of bed and rummaged through her closet in search of a robe.

It was late when they came in the night before, and Bob didn't get a good look at Jill's place. The kitchen counter was covered with greenery; ferns, miniature palm trees, and African violets all thrived and bloomed under artificial lights. While the coffee perked and brewed, Bob looked around. One room of the apartment served as an office complete with a roll-top desk, typewriter, calculator, and phone. The office, like the living room and kitchen, did second duty housing greenery.

Jill came into the kitchen wearing a bright red robe.

"It must take you hours to water these plants."

Jill poured herself a cup of coffee.

"The landlord won't allow pets."

"Don't tell me that you talk to them."

"I do. But only when I water them."

They sat at the kitchen table, drinking coffee and looking through the file Jill had assembled on Pamela Jackson. Bob was interested in the photos Jill had taken at the ranch.

"I thought it was a simple matter of doing some background on the doctor's daughter. Then I discovered that she has some strange friends."

"This guy they went out there to see looks familiar." Bob sorted through the photos again. "Let me keep these. I'll take them to the office and see what I can come up with."

They drank more coffee and looked out at the lake. An early morning fisherman was anchoring his boat near the far shore.

"Do you want me to make breakfast?"

"No." Bob glanced at his watch. "I'll be late as it is."

"You'll call?"

"You know it."

Bob gave her a long, hard kiss.

A week later, when Bob did call, Jill was sitting at her kitchen table, proofreading a report she had compiled for an insurance company. Insurance reports were Jill's principal source of income; the insurance people always wanted someone checked.

"I was beginning to think you were avoiding me," Jill said.

"Sorry, honey. I've had a thousand warrants to serve. What have you been up to."

"I've been writing reports. Are we still on for the week-end?"

"Sure thing. I thought we might go down to the Armadillo World Headquarters. You know, pretend we're young again."

"Okay."

Jill slipped the insurance report back into its file.

"Listen, I've got some information on that Jackson thing you're working on. At least I found out something about that guy in the photograph. You know, the one out at the ranch?"

"Go ahead." Jill flipped the file folder over to use as a note pad. "I'm ready."

"His name is Jimbo Bodine. He's a suspected mid-level dope dealer. DPS has a file on him from a bust they made three years ago. They stopped him coming out of the Valley with a hundred pounds of weed in the trunk of his car. He was convicted, but the case was tossed out on appeal."

"Sounds familiar."

"Anyway, I asked some people I know with the Austin PD, and as far as they can tell, Bodine's been clean since then. But I suspect that they've never looked at him close enough to catch him in action."

"Are they going to put him under surveillance?"

"No can do," Bob said. "Still no probable cause. That's how he got off last time. But we might be able to open a case if you can come up with something."

"It sounds like the girl's in deeper trouble than I thought."

"I hope the stuff on Bodine helps you out."

"I wonder if a direct approach might work? You know, go on up to Pam and start talking."

"That would certainly blow any cover you've got working for you."

"Well, I'm not making much progress playing secret agent."

"Listen, I'll call Friday and we'll decide where to go then. Get them dancing shoes ready."

"Okay," Jill said.

"And honey, be careful. These people you're watching might not be major league, but the minors are damn tough in that business."

"Don't worry about me. I'm used to tough guys. I deal with insurance people all the time."

II

It was the Saturday after Thanksgiving, and Pam was working the pay window at the parking garage when Rango and Gary stopped to visit. She was brewing Darjeeling tea on a hot plate, and the tea aroma mixed with exhaust fumes every time she slid open the pay window to collect a parking fee.

"Came by to keep you company," Rango said.

"Great. I need a break. Watch the window for me."

Gary made a start for the window, but Rango beat him to it, mounted the stool, and began collecting quarters from outgoing cars. The portable TV by the cash register played *The Rockford Files*, a new show that had become one of Pam's favorites. Another car left the garage, and Pam returned from the small bathroom at the back of the office.

"How 'bout going for a smoke?" Rango asked.

"Someone's got to watch the window."

"You two go on. I'll take care of things here."

Gary took Rango's place in the chair, and Rango and Pam walked across the garage and stepped into the elevator. There were five stories of parking at the garage, and the top level was the traditional smoking floor. The security guards never went up there.

It seemed to Gary that all Rango ever wanted to do any more was get high. Rango smoked a joint every morning before breakfast, and if he could afford to, which was most of the time, he would start using cocaine right after lunch. Rango was like some white-boy Rasta who believed he could smoke and snort his way to Zion. But for Rango, Gary decided, coke and Zion were one in the same; righteousness and spirit had nothing to do with it at all.

A car swung down the ramp from the second level of the garage and stopped at the pay gate. Gary collected the ticket and pressed the lift button, raising the barricade.

Pam had done her best to make the office homey. Hanging baskets of ivy and fern lined the high, narrow windows that looked out onto the street, and the walls of the office were decorated with Sierra Club posters.

Gary collected more tickets as cars left the garage. After a while, he began to wonder what was taking Pam and Rango so long.

Then they popped out of the elevator and walked slowly across the lot toward the office. Rango patted Pam on the shoulder, and, looking through the pay window, Gary could see but not hear them laughing. He unlocked the office door—it locked itself each time it closed—and Pam took over at the window.

Gary checked his watch and was surprised at the time. He wanted to do some Christmas shopping and had planned to do it while Pam was working. Soon the shops and vendors would be closing.

"I'm going to walk up the Drag. You want to come along?"

"No," Rango said. "I think I'll stay here and watch the tube."

Pam lifted the gate for another car; then she shut the pay window and rang up fifty cents on the cash box.

Gary left the office and walked around the Dobie Shopping Mall before turning on Guadalupe, the Drag. The afternoon was clear and sunny, but there was a chill in the breeze that blustered out of the north. Gary stayed on the campus side of the block, watching students drift in and out of the university buildings. Now that the war was over, the campus had returned to a state of normality for the first time in years.

Gary passed the Tower, the University's million volume library that was one of Austin's tallest buildings. After what Whitman had done, the Tower still made a lot of people nervous, and it sometimes affected Gary that way too even though the Tower was one of his favorite spots. He had spent many hours on the observation deck. From the deck one could see the dome of the capitol to the south, sitting among the state office buildings that dotted the city's center. To the north, the view was not so good: new industry and tracts of suburban sprawl. Low hills fringed

Austin to the west, and from the Tower some of the better homes in the town could be seen perched against the cedar-green bluffs.

For a moment, Gary thought about going up to the deck. Then he remembered that the university had closed the observation platform for the winter—too many students had taken the long leap that year. Now, with the Tower closed, the suicidal students jumped from the top of the football stadium. Some alumni had even blamed a recent loss on a kid who jumped during the game.

Gary crossed Guadalupe Street and studied the shop windows for a while, but he saw nothing that he thought Pam would like. The Drag was packed with shoppers and vendors out in full Christmas force. A woodworker sat on a canvas trap, carving toy trains and trucks from blocks of pine. Importers displayed sweaters from Oaxaca alongside African rugs with great woven slashes of red and silver running through the material. A Krishna freak dressed in long pink robes tried to sell Gary a stick of incense.

Gary stopped at a jeweler's stall and watched as she sorted out stock on her work table: bracelets of gold and silver, loose bits of polished turquoise, rings of all shapes and sizes. He thought one ring was especially beautiful. It had a pearl mounted on a gold base. Gary bought the ring thinking that it would make a good Christmas present for Pam.

In a bar called the Hole in the Wall, on the corner of Guadalupe and Twenty-fourth, Gary ordered a bourbon. The bar was a favorite of Pam's. She liked to sit at the counter, sip a Salty Dog, and stare at the cash box. The owners of the bar had placed the cash register directly beneath a giant neon dollar sign hung up on a cross, Jesus-style. Every time they rang up a sale on the register, the dollar sign would flash green.

91

That afternoon the place was jammed with students fueling up on happy-hour beer. A band of musicians played for tips and drinks. Men and women, women and women, men and men, and some persons of indeterminable sex gyrated on the small dance floor. One woman, dancing alone, swirled and thrust in white gown that was slit to her waist. She revealed a flash of blonde pubic hair with every swirl she made. Stenciled across the back of her dress in large block letters was the name of the band: VIRGIN MERRY.

Gary lit the dollar sign with an order for another Weller and water and watched the coeds drink and shake to the music. He would have to sign up for courses next semester, Gary thought. When the draft had ended, he had dropped out of college and taken the liquor store job to earn some money. Now college seemed possible again. He had put off returning to school for too long. He sucked the last drops of bourbon from the ice cubes, went out onto the street, and headed for the parking garage.

With sundown it had turned even cooler. Along Guadalupe couples walked arm in arm, bundled against the descending night. On one street corner a woman played a flute, ringing melancholy notes off the empty university buildings.

Gary knew something was wrong when he saw a car pull out of the parking garage without stopping at the pay window. It was much too early for Pam to have closed up shop, but the exit gate was up and the office was dark. Gary went up the drive to the window and peered inside. The room was almost black behind the tinted security glass. Then he saw them on the floor, their bodies like white shadows. Pam was on top.

Gary rode the elevator to the roof of the garage, looked out on the city as it lit up for the night, then tossed the ring to the street below. For a long while he stayed on the roof of the garage, staring over the building's edge and enjoying the sobering effect of the wind flushing his face. He fought back his anger and his pain in that way he learned to do when his parents had been killed in Mexico.

Finally, he took the elevator down to the third level where he had parked the Mustang. The pay gate was still up when he drove out at about thirty miles per hour. He turned on Guadalupe, missed a parked car by a couple of inches, then slowed and made a turn toward Lamar.

At Chris' store, he bought a quart of Weller and a bag of ice. Chris was in a good mood, smiling like a millionaire. He was always happy when sales were going well, and he was ready for the busy holiday season. The store was done up with Christmas displays, decorated with lights and flags and a life-sized cardboard cut-out of the Black Velvet Blonde cradling a bottle of Canadian whiskey between her breasts.

"Hey." Chris bagged the bottle of bourbon. "You look pretty down. What's the problem?"

"It's nothing a good drunk won't cure."

"There's no such thing as a good drunk. What's the matter? Money trouble? You can always work more hours for me. I'll even make you manager."

"Thanks, Chris, but it's not about money."

"I see. You got girl trouble, don't you?"

"Yeah."

"I've got the cure."

Chris reached down to the bottom shelf of the liqueur rack, produced a bottle of ouzo, and handed it to Gary.

"Ever tried this?"

"No, I never heard of it."

"It's the Greek love juice. You and your girl split this bottle, and I promise you'll be back in love."

"How much is it?"

"For you, free. A Christmas present."

"Thanks, Chris. You're a good pal."

"Now go on home. Everything will work out. You'll see."

Gary went out of the store and was fumbling for the keys to the car when he noticed the Cougar convertible. The car looked vaguely familiar to him, as did the brunette behind the wheel. She saw him looking at her and she smiled. She got out of the car.

"Gary, I hope you realize that Pam needs help."

Gary gave the brunette a hard look. She was about ten years older than he; she was tall, with dark eyes to match her hair, and she wore a white sweater and green wool skirt.

"What are you talking about? Who are you? How do you know my name?"

"My name's Jill. Jill McDaniel. You don't know me, but I'm a friend."

"A friend, huh. Whose friend?"

"I'd like to be your friend." Jill put on her most innocent look. "I was hired by Pam's father. He's very worried about her."

"Great. That's great."

"You're heading for trouble, you know? I mean, if you don't steer clear of Jimbo Bodine, things will end up badly for all of you."

"I don't know what the hell you're talking about, lady." Gary opened the door of his car.

Jill smiled.

"Look, I don't know who you are, a cop I'd guess, but I don't much care. And if you're really working for Pam's father, then you know what an asshole he is. So let us alone."

He started up the car and Jill came closer to the driver's window. She took her business card from the pocket of her skirt.

"Here." She gave the card to Gary. "My number's there. You can call anytime you want to talk. Remember, I only want to help."

Gary looked at the card a moment.

>Jill McDaniel
>Research and Investigations
>Fully Licensed and Bonded
>512-521-4039

"Yeah, sure." Gary stuffed the card in his shirt pocket and put the car in reverse.

"Call me."

Gary backed the car out of its parking place and sped off down Lamar Street.

There was no one home, so Gary poured himself a glass of ouzo and waited for Pam to return. Midnight came, then one o'clock, and Gary still waited, drinking the funny Greek liqueur and thinking about Jill McDaniel and the card she had given him. Finally, he passed out on the couch, too drunk on ouzo to make it to the bedroom.

The next morning he woke in bed with Pam curled against him. He lay still awhile, luxuriating in Pam's body heat as Pam yawned and stirred.

"You must feel awful this morning."

She stretched and gave Gary a kiss on the neck.

"We found you on the floor with a half empty bottle next to you," Pam said. "You missed a great midnight movie: *The Harder They Come*. That reggae singer, Jimmy Cliff, is in it."

She snuggled closer against him and began to stroke his penis. Then his hangover took control, and he staggered up from the bed and made a dash for the bathroom. After a few minutes he stumbled back into the room and collapsed on the bed.

"Poor baby. It's not like you to get so soused."

Gary shook his head.

"None of us have been acting much like ourselves," he said.

"What's that supposed to mean?"

"I mean I know about you and Rango. I saw you screwing him last evening at the garage."

Pam bounced off the bed, stood, and stretched. Then she picked up a hair brush from the dresser and started brushing her long hair.

"I guess I knew you'd find out sooner or later."

"Remember when you broke it off with that guy in Leaky Seals? You promised you'd never do that to me again."

Gary watched the mirror for a reflection of her face that would cue him to what she was thinking. But Pam stood there in the nude, stroking the brush through her blonde hair and looking as content as some beautiful female Buddha.

"I'm sorry."

Pam left the room, and when Gary heard her turn on the shower, he crawled out of bed and put on a pair of jeans. He was surprised to find Rango sitting in the den and chopping on his morning cocaine. Gary plopped down in the chair across from him, but Rango didn't look up from his work.

"Try a line of this. It'll fix your head."

"No thanks."

Rango continued to play with his cocaine, and Gary got up and rummaged through the beer bottles in the refrigerator till he found a can of tomato juice. Rango was pinching his nostrils together when Gary dropped back down in the chair, cradling his juice in both hands.

Rango flipped through a stack of albums until he found one he liked, Kinky Friedman's *Sold American*. Gary wondered how long Rango and Pam had been screwing each other, and he wondered too if he had really met a beautiful woman cop the night before or if she had been part of an ouzo of a dream.

Pam came out of the bedroom dressed in blue jeans and the white Oaxacan wedding shirt that Gary had bought for her the summer they had gone to Mexico together. She was still toweling off her hair as she sat down on the couch by Rango.

"He knows about us," Pam said.

"You told him?"

"No, I saw you together last night. At the garage."

No one said a word as Pam drove down the interstate to Sixth Street. Pam and Rango seemed to be taking the situation so casually that Gary was beginning to feel guilty about letting his middle-class pain show through.

Mexicans in work clothes crowded every table in the front room of Cisco's. Gary often thought that the owner paid them to sit there all day, drinking coffee and lending some atmosphere to the place. The cafe was clouded with the smoke and smell of cooking sausage and burning cigarettes. Rango led them though the kitchen, and they took a table in the back dining room. Pictures of famous Texans dotted the paneled walls; Gary sat under a photo of LBJ. There were a few other people in the dining room: students and business types getting a late breakfast. The waiter came and took the order; everyone wanted migas, scrambled eggs and sausage.

"You weren't even going to tell me, were you?"

Pam lit a cigarette.

97

"I would have gotten around to it eventually."

Her eyes were hard and unflinching.

"I don't know how it happened," Rango said. "It seemed natural."

"Yeah, real natural."

"Gary," Pam said, "it was my fault. I started it, but . . ."

"But what?"

"But I didn't mean to hurt you. That's all."

Gary didn't say anything. He had been through this before when Pam had her affair with the singer in the Leaky Seals band. Pam forked her eggs into a little pile but didn't taste them.

"This is one reason I didn't tell you. I knew you'd get upset."

Gary stared at her.

"If you want to pretend nothing's changed, then I can play it that way, too."

"It's not like I quit sleeping with you," Pam said.

"That's mighty sweet of you, baby."

Gary splashed some coffee out of his cup as he sat it down. Rango smiled. He was enjoying the situation.

Late that afternoon, Pam went to work at the garage, so Gary had the house to himself. He went to the bedroom, turned on the television, and lay down. It was time for *Dr. Bill's*. He had never met Dr. Jackson, but Pam told some stories about how her father badgered her mother past the breaking point, to the drinking point. And Pam mentioned that the year before she left home for college, her father had always seemed to appear whenever she decided to take a shower. She had been quick to add that her father had never touched her, that he had only looked at her in a troubling way.

Seeing Dr. Jackson parade across the television screen

troubled Gary, too. If Jill McDaniel was working for Dr. Jackson, what could it mean? Could the old man really have some love for his daughter? Maybe Pam had misjudged her father.

It seemed clear to Gary that he only had two choices. He could either stay and play along with the insanity Pam was determined to put him through, or he could pack and go. He knew he couldn't leave. A little Pam was better than no Pam at all. Besides, Gary told himself, Pam never stuck with anything. Once she finished her fling with Rango, she would settle down to what passed with her for normal. For now, he would do nothing. He would go along with Pam and Rango. He would keep quiet about the woman who was spying on them. If they could make it till spring, maybe they could take a trip, get away from Rango. Maybe they would go to Alaska. Gary could almost see them on the ferry, making love all the way up the Inside Passage.

Pam woke him by pulling at the hair on his chest and sucking on his nipples.

"Don't worry, baby," she whispered. "I still love you."

She stroked his skin with a touch so soft that for a moment he thought he was dreaming. Then Pam began to kiss her way down his body, moving all the way to his toes and then starting back up again. They concluded their fight as they concluded every fight they had ever had, with a long, slow session of love making. And as Gary clung to Pam, he wondered if she could do anything that would make him leave. When you're afraid of losing someone you love, you start to love them even more.

Bob Maran's office was located in a strip shopping center on Austin's far north side. The county had rented a storefront next to a Petland and a Magic Wok shop, and

Bob shared his building with a justice of the peace and a license plate renewal station. Jill parked her car and went into the building. Inside, several people were lined up in front of a counter, waiting for their new license plates. Jill made her way to the wing that housed the county offices, and a gray- haired receptionist took her name and announced her presence to Bob via the intercom.

"His office is at the end of the hall."

Jill walked down the well-lit hallway. Deputies dressed in dark blue uniforms wandered in and out of the offices. The hall was decorated with a long bulletin board covered with wanted posters and official memoranda.

Bob greeted Jill at the door of his office and then offered her a chair across from his desk. There was a United States flag on one side of the room, and a Texas flag graced the opposite corner. Jill thought that Bob's desk looked suspiciously neat; completely clear of paper work, the desktop held only a yellow legal pad and a black phone.

"Either you cleaned off your desk for my visit or constables don't have enough to do."

"Your coming by did give me an excuse to straighten up the place a bit. We're not too formal around here, but I like to run a neat shop. At least I try to keep the office in better shape than the Petland next door."

"I'll never get used to these branch courthouses."

"Actually, I'm glad to be out here. At least I've got a building with decent air conditioning. The downtown courthouse is really getting dumpy."

"Are we still on for lunch?"

"Sure," Bob said.

"Let me fill you in on the Bodine-Jackson case first."

"What more have you found out?"

"Bodine's left his ranch, best as I can tell. His caretaker's still on guard, but I didn't spot anyone else at his place."

"Might be they're running a deal."

"I don't know."

"Have you talked to the girl's father?"

"I've called his office several times, but he's never in. He does keep sending me my check, though. A thousand a month, like clockwork. So every week I type up a report, a couple of pages on Pam's activities, and send it up to Dallas."

Bob doodled on the yellow legal pad. "Sounds to me like this Dr. Jackson is an odd bird, a rich one too it seems. Of course, he must care something for his daughter or he wouldn't pay you to watch her."

"When I talked to him in Dallas it was more like he wanted to be certain Pam wouldn't disgrace him with some scandal. The good doctor is very ambitious, you know."

"I'll help out anyway I can. But if they are dealing, do you want the girl busted, too?"

Jill considered it a moment.

"I hope she's not involved in that. Really, we've got no proof that Jimbo Bodine is operating a drug ring."

Bob tore the page of paper from the legal pad and started doodling on a fresh sheet.

"I'll bet we could dig up some dirt there if we looked hard enough. People like Bodine never change. He's managed to get some money somewhere, and he doesn't seem to have a regular job. He's probably a small fish, but we could fry him if we wanted."

The phone on his desk rang, and he answered it and began taking notes on the legal pad in between yeses and okays. Then he hung up the phone and turned back to Jill.

"A law man's work is never done. We'll have to skip that lunch today."

"Guess I'll have to settle for a rain check."

"I'm really sorry."

"There is one thing I haven't told you because I know you won't approve. I confronted Pam's boyfriend, the one named Gary, and I told him that I was working for Pam's father."

"What did Gary say then?"

"He thought I was a cop."

Bob chewed on the end of his pen a moment and considered the problem.

"Then that might also explain why they've suddenly left town. Maybe they're hiding out."

"Could be."

"Well, we don't have enough on Bodine to get a search warrant, but I could start a file on him. Since he lives in Travis County, he falls into my jurisdiction. We can do a little work on it together, if you want. Besides, there's some nice hill-country motels out that way we can explore."

Jill blushed.

"Constable, you're shameless."

III

Bob Maran sighed and handed the binoculars to Jill. She held the glasses to her eyes and scanned the ranch below for some sign of activity. The field between the house and the stream was covered with bluebonnets that rippled in the warm south wind, and the oaks and cottonwoods that bordered the creek were thick and green, flush with spring.

"When I was here last fall there was a party going on, and Jimbo was shooting pigeons."

"Pigeons?"

"Pigeons," Jill said. "It's about replaced trapshooting, at least for the wealthy. Instead of clay birds, they use real pigeons. You know, release them from cages then shoot them out of the air."

"There doesn't seem to be anyone down there now."

"Hold on. There's the guard."

Jill handed the binoculars back to Bob. Bob took the field glasses and focused on the man as he came out of the house. He was a tall, wide-shouldered fellow with a big revolver holstered to his hip. He walked slowly toward the creek that skirted the base of the cliff, a fishing pole in one hand and a tackle box in the other.

"This guy packs a lot of firepower on his fishing trips. He's worried about something. But there's no telling." Bob watched the man through the binoculars. "These people don't operate on logic. Druggies tend to believe in luck, or karma, or some sort of superstition."

Bob put the field glasses in their leather case, and then he and Jill crawled away from the edge of the cliff. They stood up, and Jill tucked her shirt into her jeans. They strolled across the pasture, cutting through the blue-bonnets and Indian paints that colored the rocky land with soft hues of blue and pink.

Finally they reached the fence and the road and Jill's car. Bob helped Jill crawl under the barbed wire; then he climbed the fence and put the binoculars in the trunk.

"It probably was a mistake to approach Gary," Jill said. "But I was getting nowhere following them around Austin. Besides, I had to do something."

"Drugs will change those kids. They won't respect anything after a while. They'll turn on each other, forget that they were ever friends. I've seen it happen before."

"It seems like a different world from when we were in school. I guess it was the war that changed everything."

"Now there are no rules. If it feels good, do it. Hell, it's the ethos of the age."

Jill gave him a funny look as she got into the car.

"Ethos of the age. That's pretty fancy talking for a college dropout."

Bob used his hat to brush the dust from his uniform; then he climbed into the passenger's seat and laughed.

"Didn't I tell you? I finished my degree at the University of Houston. Went to school while I was a cop."

"Really?" Jill started the engine and pulled onto the road. "I'm impressed. What was your major?"

"Sociology. They taught us all the right words there. Take the next left."

"Here?" Jill slowed the Cougar down.

"Yeah, here."

Jill turned off the blacktop and onto a gravel drive. The road twisted across a pasture and disappeared into a small valley that was secluded by cedar trees.

"This is something else I forgot to tell you."

He opened his briefcase and produced some neatly folded legal papers.

"I've got to serve a peace bond on the fellow that lives at the end of this drive. This guy's a good old Bubba who won't let his estranged wife be."

Jill slowed the Cougar and dodged a large pothole.

"What's his name?"

"Bullhead. Bullhead Jones. I've been out here before. He likes to slap his old lady around a bit. Got himself arrested a couple of times before the gal decided that she'd had enough. But he keeps showing up at his mother-in-law's house in Austin."

"Bullhead. How'd he get name like that?"

"He's called Bullhead because he's a catfish doodler."

"Catfish doodler?"

"Doodling is a peculiar sport. The way they do it around here is to wade into the river when the water's low. Catfish like hollow logs, and when the doodler finds a likely log, he reaches into it and wrestles out a catfish with his bare hands. Jones doodled a fifty pound bullhead out of the Colorado River a few years back, and that's how he got his name."

"How do they know that there's not a snake in the hollow log?"

"They don't know. But that's considered part of the sport. In fact, there's a story about one doodler who reached into a nest of water moccasins. He had a dozen snakes on his arm when he pulled it out of that log. Poor fellow was dead before they could get him out of the river."

They had crossed the pasture, and as the road started to dip into the draw, Jill spotted a mobile home planted at the foot of the small hills.

"This Bullhead, is he dangerous?"

"Not unless you marry him. He's crazy drunk most all the time."

"Do you have to do this sort of thing often?"

"I usually leave these jobs for the deputies. But I knew we'd be out this way, so I figured I might as well take care if it myself."

"So that's why you're wearing a uniform today."

"Yeah, I don't like it much. But when I've got to serve papers on a man like Bullhead, it helps to remind him of the force of the law."

Bullhead was sitting on the front porch of his mobile home when Jill pulled up in the yard and parked next to an old pickup truck that had its hood up. Jill had imagined Bullhead to be a fat, beer-bellied redneck, but the man was thin and wiry with a long, frizzy back beard that hung down on his chest as he leaned back in his lawn chair. There was a .22 rifle propped against the mobile home, and two freshly killed rabbits lay bleeding on the porch. Bullhead remained seated, a can of beer in one hand, while Jill turned off the engine.

Bob unsnapped the strap that secured his .38 service revolver in its holster.

"You stay in the car. This shouldn't take but a minute."

"Hey there, Bullhead." Bob got out of the car. "See you've been doing a little hunting."

"Yeap," he said.

Bullhead leaned back in his chair and raised the beer to his lips. His arms were striped with thin, purple scars, reminders of the big catfish he had handled. He finished off the brew before crushing the can and casually tossing it onto a heap of empties that cluttered the porch behind him.

"Done got enough for dinner, anyhow."

"You know why I'm here?"

"I ain't none nothing you can arrest me for."

Bullhead reached into his shirt pocket and produced a plug of chewing tobacco. Then he snapped open his pocketknife, cut a chew, and held the plug out toward Bob.

"You want a chaw?"

"Thanks, but I'll pass."

Bob stepped up onto the porch and handed the legal papers to Bullhead.

"Now Bullhead, this is a Peace Bond I'm serving you with. It says for you to keep away from that wife of yours, and if you give her or her mother any trouble, if you go showing up at their place, I'll have to take you in."

Bullhead took the papers from Bob and unfolded them. He glanced at the clean white pages and neat typing as if he were examining an artifact from another world.

"I was drunk last time. I don't want no trouble with the law."

"You're drunk every time. We don't want trouble either.

But this is your last warning. If I have to come out here again, it'll be to arrest you."

"Don't worry. You won't hear about me no more."

"Good enough." Bob stepped down from the porch and started walking toward Jill's car. "You stay clear of that woman, you hear?'

"You got my word." Bullhead tucked the legal papers into his shirt pocket.

Bob got back into the Cougar, and Jill started the engine. Bullhead got up from his chair, stared at Jill a moment, then leaned across the porch railing and spit a brown stream of tobacco into the yard.

"He's a high-class fellow."

Jill turned the car around in the yard and started back toward the highway.

"Yeah. But there are worse."

Jill drove them south, through the hill country toward Canyon Lake and the Guadalupe River. Patches of bluebonnets and Indian paints decorated the roadside, and the cedar trees dotted the rocky hills.

"I knew we'd have a pretty spring this year."

"How's that?" Jill kept her eyes on the road.

"All that rain last fall. That's what determines how many wild flowers will bloom."

"My mother loved wild flowers. She knew the proper names for them all."

"When did she die?" Bob asked.

"Seven years ago. After she died, Dad decided to retire from his law practice and move to California. He lives in San Francisco with his new wife now."

"He married again, did he?"

"Yes, to a nice woman who's only forty-five years old. I went to visit them last year. I think my mother would have been happy that Dad found someone. Her name's Sally.

She's a nurse."

They rode along silently for a few miles. Jill watched the road, and Bob stared out the window as the rough land rolled away.

"Both of my folks are still alive. They sold the hardware store and moved to Colorado. They were tired of hot summers, I guess. I see them a couple of times a year. They seem happy up there."

"That's good." Jill glanced at Bob. "I liked your folks."

"They liked you, too. My mother hoped we'd get married."

"Really? Your mother was always sweet to me."

While Jill drove along, Bob opened his briefcase and took out a clean, white shirt and a pair of neatly folded blue jeans.

"Once we cross the county line, I'm officially off duty. It's time to put on the civilian clothes."

He took off his uniform shirt and unbuckled his holster. After he stuffed his service revolver into the briefcase, he put on the fresh white shirt and began to unzip his trousers.

"Keep your eyes on the road, darling," Bob slipped out of his pants. "I hate to be in a wreck while I've got my pants down."

"Don't worry officer. I can control myself until we get to the motel."

Bob laughed and finished changing clothes. They came to an intersection and stopped for the blinking red light. The road forked, one way leading to Canyon Lake and another to the town of Sattler. Jill took the turn for Sattler, where Bob said he knew of a good motel that overlooked the river.

Right before they reached town, the road bridged the Guadalupe, a blue-green ribbon of water bordered by tall cypress trees.

"The motel's on the right."

A moment later Jill spotted the sign: HORSESHOE FALLS MOTEL—ROOMS ON THE RIVER.

"Do you take all your girl friends here?"

"Only the ones that like white water. I discovered this place when I used to canoe the river."

Jill pulled up in front of the motel and Bob went into the office to register for a room. In only a few minutes he returned with a key. It was the middle of the week, and still too early for the vacation crowds that filled the place during the summer months, so they had the motel mostly to themselves. Their room was at the far end of the building, a few yards from the river's edge. Bob unlocked the room and then helped Jill carry in their bags.

"Well?" Jill put her suitcase down next to the bed and smiled. "What's it going to be first? A swim or me?"

Bob grinned and pulled the door shut behind him.

Jill thought that Bob was asleep. He wasn't snoring, like he sometimes did, but he was very still and quiet and warm against her. The light that seeped through the drawn curtains was slowly fading with the afternoon. Bob groaned and shifted his leg. A long, thin scar ran up his calf. Jill reached out to touch him, instinctively running a finger across the scar.

"It's ugly, isn't it?"

He had opened one eye, but that had been his only movement.

"Not really." Jill was a little bit embarrassed.

Bob got out of bed and went to the bathroom. When he returned he was wearing a shirt and a pair of jeans.

Jill propped her head up with a pillow.

"Tell me how you got hurt."

"There's not much to tell." Bob sat down on the edge of the bed. "It was in Houston. I was working the late shift, alone, of course." Bob reached under the bed for his boots, and he started to put them on. "Anyway, I was patrolling a street that had a lot of ice houses, bars we'd call them here, when I saw a car weaving across the center line. So I pulled the guy over. He was a Mexican, a young guy. I asked for his driver's license. He reached into his pocket and came out with a .25 auto. The little bastard fired three shots before his gun jammed. One shot hit the pavement, but I took two in the leg."

Bob finished putting on his boots.

"So, what happened next?"

"The funny thing about it is that I didn't even know I'd been shot. When his gun jammed, I punched that kid in the face. I dragged him out of the car and cuffed him and radioed for some backup. By then I was bleeding like a pig. Anyway, three squad cars came and hauled the Mexican to jail while an ambulance arrived for me."

"Why did he shoot you?"

"He was a crazy, drunk, illegal. I guess he didn't want to go to jail. Hell, I don't know what he was worried about. They finally did send him to Huntsville, but I heard later that he only served six months before they deported him."

"And that's when you quit?"

"That was one reason. Houston was the other. That town's a real mess."

"So you moved home to Austin and ran for constable?"

"Right. But enough of this history. Let's go get some barbeque."

"Can I get dressed first?"

"Only if you hurry. I'm starving."

The first thing Rango and Gary noticed when they

turned back into the drive at the house in the Avenues was the black Volvo. The car could only belong to one person: Pam's father, Dr. Jackson. They got out of the car and walked up to the front porch. Gary knocked on the door, and after a moment Pam answered.

"Come on in. Everybody's here now."

Gary and Rango went into the den, and Dr. Jackson got up from his place on the couch. Gary was a bit surprised to see that Dr. Jackson was only about five-foot six. On television, the doctor always seemed tall.

"Daddy, I want you to meet my friends. This is Rango, and that's Gary, the boy I told you about."

Doctor Jackson glared at Rango and Gary.

"I won't pretend to like either of you," Doctor Jackson said.

Pam blushed.

"Please," she said.

"No, I won't stop. I know the entire disgusting story. Is that how your mother and I raised you?"

"Don't bring her into this, Daddy."

"Oh, don't worry. I'm not going to recount our family troubles in the presence of these two." Doctor Jackson nodded toward Gary and Rango. "I came here to take you home to Dallas, to help you start to make something of your life."

"Daddy, why are you doing this? I haven't done anything wrong."

"Young lady," Dr. Jackson said, "that statement only proves how much you need my help. Now are you coming with me or not?"

Pam stared down at the floor. Gary and Rango gave each other a quick look.

"Don't pretend you care," Pam said. "You're only worried that I might embarrass you. If that happened, then your stupid television show might be forced off the air."

Doctor Jackson walked to the door, passing Gary and Rango without even looking at them.

"When you want help, not money, but help putting your life back together, you know where to call."

Gary, Pam, and Rango stood in the room and listened as the Volvo's engine started and raced and the car pulled off down the street.

"Nice guy, your dad." Rango ginned.

"Oh, shut up."

Pam walked to the bedroom and slammed the door shut behind her.

It was shortly after Dr. Jackson's visit that Pam decided a move was in order. She didn't want her father to show up unexpectedly again. After a couple of days of looking, she located a lake house that was for rent. Pam and Gary wanted the place the moment they saw it. The house sat atop a bluff overlooking the water, and the real estate lady explained that the owner was working out of the country for a year. That explained the reasonable rent.

It was a large house with three bedrooms which all had picture windows that looked out onto Lake Travis. There was a dining room full of early American furniture and a living room with a polished pink granite floor and a high ceiling that was spanned by oak beams. Out back was a redwood patio complete with redwood tables and chairs, and because the house was at the very top of the bluff, the hills could be seen rolling away in the west behind the lake. A steel-cage elevator was ready to carry passengers down the side of the bluff to the lake's shore where a strip of grass about ten yards wide bordered the water and where there was a boathouse, but no boat.

Gary and Pam spent a few more nights at the house in

the Avenues, and during the days they shuttled back and forth to the lake with loads of stuff packed into the Mustang. The morning after they unpacked the last box of books and put away all their clothes, they sat on the patio, drinking coffee and watching the boats cut across the lake.

"I love it."

"What?" Gary asked.

"Everything. The house, the lake, the hills."

"And me?"

"And you."

Pam finished her coffee and put on a pair of blue cutoffs and a yellow tee-shirt. Then Gary led her out of the house and across the patio to the elevator.

"What's going on?"

Gary closed the elevator's gate and started them down to the lake.

"You'll see."

They reached the bottom of the cliff and got out of the elevator. It was only a short walk across the close-cut lawn to the water and the boathouse.

"Go on." Gary pointed to the boathouse. "Look inside."

Pam went inside, stayed a moment, and then came running out. Gary had never seen her as happy as she looked then, standing there on the lawn, barefoot and smiling.

"When did you get it?"

"They delivered it this morning while you were still sleeping."

"Really, you bought it for me?"

"And it's fully loaded, too. Your boat, as they say, has finally come in. It's outfitted for skiing and bass fishing."

"How can you afford it?"

"I finally got access to some of the money my folks left me," Gary said. "I quit the liquor store, too. Chris didn't like that much."

"Can we take it out?"

Gary reached into his jeans pocket and fished out the boat keys; then he tossed the keys to Pam.

"You drive. I'll show you the ropes."

That evening Rango, Pam, and Gary sat on the patio, enjoying the breeze that came in off the lake. The sun had gone down, but the western sky was still fringed with pink light that silhouetted the hills on the horizon. Gary struggled with the adjustment on the new charcoal grill he had bought for the occasion.

"You got a good sunburn out there today," Rango said.

He was right about that. Pam and Gary had spent six straight hours in the boat, skiing and fishing. Pam even dusted off her fly rod, and Gary practically forced her to come in that evening so they could start dinner and get ready for the concert at the Armadillo World Headquarters.

Rango chopped out some cocaine on his pocket mirror and passed it over to Pam.

"You hear anything from Jimbo?"

"I guess he's still in Houston. Who knows what he's up to. He doesn't exactly advertise his whereabouts."

Finally Gary got the grill level and the fire right: white hot. He tossed the steaks on the grill and they sizzled up in flames before Gary poured half a beer on the fire.

"How about you?" Pam asked. "What have you been doing?"

"I've been busy making money," Rango said.

Gary went across the patio and got a fresh beer out of the ice chest.

"I think you're crazy to keep dealing."

"Well, I think you're crazy not to get in on all the dough."

After dinner they packed into the Mustang and headed into Austin for the show at the Armadillo. The beer garden behind the building was full of people talking and drinking in the warm night air, and there was a long line waiting to buy tickets.

The Armadillo World Headquarters was easily the strangest music hall in the state. Once it had been owned by the National Guard, and it was really nothing more than a large tin building with a high roof and a stage at one end. There were no chairs inside the Armadillo, forcing everyone to sit on the floor or stand at the bar. But the Armadillo was justly famous as the home of some of the hottest music in the Southwest.

In addition to hosting Rock and Country bands, the 'Dillo was the birthplace of the odd, underground effort to establish the armadillo as the official state animal of Texas. In fact, a local artist had recently painted a mural on one side of the building; the mural portrayed a giant armadillo attempting to mate with the dome of the capitol building. Most of the supporters of the armadillo uprising realized the battle was hopeless. There was no way the football fans and rednecks of Texas would allow a scavenger animal to represent the Lone Star State, not when a longhorn could do the job. And a lot of the old timers thought that the idea of making the armadillo the state animal was downright distasteful. These were folks who had lived through the Depression and who still called armadillos "Hoover Hogs." All armadillos reminded them of was indigestion. There was even a rumor going around Austin that the Armadillo World Headquarters itself was in danger of extinction: a group of bankers wanted to tear it down and turn it into a parking lot.

As they paid for their tickets, a street freak tugged at Pam's shoulder and begged for a handout. The kid couldn't have been older than sixteen, but he had yellow eyes from sniffing paint or glue. His clothes were caked with dirt and sweat, and he smelled about as good as the vote count in LBJ's first election to Congress.

"Bug off, amigo," Rango said to the kid.

"No, wait."

She reached into the pocket of her jeans and took out a thin fold of bills. She separated a twenty from the rest and gave it to the kid. He mumbled his thanks, looked at the bill, looked at Pam again, then turned and ran.

Jill McDaniel and Bob Maran were sitting at a table in a corner of the beer garden when the boy ran through the crowd and pushed his way out into the parking lot. That was when Bob first noticed that Pam, Gary, and Rango were standing in line, waiting to enter the Armadillo. He and Jill stopped by the beer garden after going out to dinner. They were talking, enjoying the evening breeze, and watching the crowd assemble for the concert.

"Look there."

Bob gave Jill a nudge with his elbow.

"What?"

"In the line, up towards the front. It's your client's daughter, Pam."

"She's got both her boyfriends with her tonight."

Bob took a sip of his beer. He wasn't much of a drinker, but he had to admit that a frosty mug of Shiner went well with the warm Texas evening.

"You still getting paid to look after her?"

"Not as of last week. I got my last thousand dollar check in the mail, along with a letter from the good doctor thanking me for my services and explaining that my help was no longer needed. I knew that gravy train was too good to last."

"I still think you were on to something with Jimbo Bodine." Bob poured them each another beer from the pitcher. "I know he's dealing."

Jill sipped her beer and watched as the line started to move and Gary, Pam, and Rango went into the dance hall.

"Oh, we're right about Bodine," Jill said. "I can't prove it either, but he's a hood for sure. I don't think these kids are all that bad though. They're mixed up, got in a bit over their heads, is all."

"I don't know about that. But I wish someone would give me a tip on Bodine. I haven't made a good bust all month."

"All month?" Jill laughed. "I happen to know that the most exciting thing you've done all year was serve a warrant on Bullhead Jones."

"Ah, come on."

"Talking about tips, though, if anyone would know what Jimbo was up to, Pam's boyfriends would. Maybe I could convince them to give us some information."

"How would you get them to do that?"

"I could confront Gary again. I could tell him they were in line to be busted, unless he decides to help us. He thinks I'm a cop anyway."

"Of course, I really couldn't make that kind of a deal."

"Yes, but Gary won't know that. All he'll know is that if he doesn't help us get Jimbo, then he and Pam will go to jail."

Bob took a long sip of beer and a smiled.

"Honey, you'd make a clever little narcotics officer."

Inside, the Armadillo was dark and crowded, and it took a moment for Pam, Gary, and Rango to find a spot of floor space where they could sit. The dance hall wasn't all that large, and the stage could be seen from anywhere in the place. The trick was to sit somewhere out of the line of traffic so that nobody kicked over your beer. The next trick was to be close to the bar in case somebody did kick over your beer. Rango and Gary left Pam to guard their places while they pushed their way to the bar where a long line of thirsty young people had formed.

While they waited for their pitchers, Rango put his arm around Gary's shoulder.

"Amigo." Rango had to yell to be heard over the noise of the crowd. "I owe you one. I shouldn't have given you so much shit about Pam."

Gary gave Rango a hard look.

"No, I mean it. I fucked up. But I'm telling you, she asked for it. I swear."

The bartender handed Gary a full pitcher of beer and started to draw a second one.

"Forget it." Gary passed the pitcher to Rango. "It's not the first time you've messed up. But make sure it's the last, *comprendes?*"

"*Comprendo.*"

IV

It was only a few days later when Rango called long distance from La Grange wanting Pam and Gary to get him out of jail. They had been out on the lake all afternoon and had put away the boat and ridden the elevator to the house when the phone rang. Gary could tell that Rango had run into some bad trouble; there was a trace of panic in his voice.

"Listen, they popped me down here for coke. You got to come and get me out."

"Jesus, what happened?"

"I'll tell you later. Come and get me."

Then there was a click on the line and the connection

went dead.

"What is it?"

Pam stood in the doorway with her hands full of fishing gear and her hair still wet from her last swim.

"Rango's been arrested. He's in the county jail down in La Grange. We're supposed to get him out."

"Damn it," Pam said. "I told him it would happen."

"I'm going to call Jimbo and ask about a lawyer."

Gary dialed Jimbo's number, and after about twenty rings, Bodine answered his phone.

"Jimbo?"

"Yeah, who's this?"

"This is Gary. Rango's friend. We've got a problem. We're going to need some help."

"What is it?"

"Rango's in jail. Down in La Grange."

Jimbo coughed.

"What's the charge?"

"They got him with some coke."

Jimbo sighed into the phone. Gary could almost feel him thinking on the other end of the line.

"I guess we'd better get him out before he slips and says something stupid."

"What do you want us to do?"

"One of you'll have to pick Rango up. I know a lawyer in Houston that will meet you with the bail money. Better send that girl Pam. The cops will think it's his girl friend. And have her circle back through San Antonio or something, in case the police put a tail on them."

"I knew you wouldn't let us down."

"I'm covering my own ass. Now get Pam on the road."

"Okay."

"And one more thing. I don't want you or Rango calling me anymore. Tell Rango that I'll be in touch with him in a few days."

"I understand."

Gary hung up the phone and turned to face Pam. She was still standing at the doorway.

"Jimbo wants you to drive down and pick up Rango."

"Why me?"

"He thinks it'll look less suspicious if a woman goes to get him. You don't have to do anything illegal. Drive down to La Grange and pick Rango up. Jimbo said to come back by way of San Antonio in case you're being followed."

"San Antonio! That's hours out of the way."

"Look. Jimbo's afraid they'll make Rango talk if we can't get him out tonight. Do you want him to end up in Huntsville?"

Pam turned away and went into the bedroom. Fifteen minutes later she was dressed and ready to go.

Pam and Rango didn't make it back to the lake house until the next evening. Pam claimed that when they reached San Antonio, they were too tired to drive anymore so they got a room and slept a few hours. This didn't make Gary very happy, but he ignored the explanation and tried not to think of Pam and Rango together somewhere in a motel.

"It was pure bad luck," Rango said.

They were sitting out on the patio, drinking beers and watching the stars blaze away in the hill country sky. There was a full moon rising, and they could make out the humps of hills beyond the lake.

"I told you it would happen." Pam waved her cigarette at Rango.

Rango sipped at his beer.

"It was a freak thing. I was on my way to Houston with some coke I've been trying to unload. I had it all tucked away in the trunk, nice and safe. I stopped right out of La Grange at this antique shop. I wasn't in the place ten minutes. I looked around, bought a pack of cigarettes, and left. That's it."

Rango finished off his beer and popped the top on another one.

"Next thing I know, there's a DPS patrol car on my ass, flashing lights and all. Wasn't much I could do except pull over, but with the dope all locked up in the trunk I wasn't really too worried. Seems the cops stopped me because the shopkeeper back at the antique store reported that I'd stolen something.

"When I wouldn't open the trunk the cops got pissed. They took my keys and opened it themselves. They thought they'd find something I'd shoplifted, and they came up with my stash."

"I thought they had to have a warrant."

"That's what I told them. They claimed they had cause to suspect that I was in possession of stolen property."

They were all quiet for a few minutes. An owl hooted down by the lake. The moon slipped behind a wisp of high clouds, then reappeared bright and yellow.

"What was the La Grange jail like?"

Rango blew a chain of smoke rings off his cigarette.

"I was ready to spend the night, you know. But when they close that door behind you and you look around at nothing but steel bunks and concrete, then you know that you can't even imagine what ten years in Huntsville would be like."

"God," Pam said. "Ten years?"

"The State of Texas is not real fond of cocaine dealers."

"What are you going to do if that happens, if you get a long sentence?" Gary asked.

Rango shrugged. "They won't take me alive."

A few weeks later, Pam, Rango, and Gary were again at the lake house, but instead of worrying about Rango doing jail time, they were celebrating his legal victory. Rango didn't have to run; Jimbo's money and help were all it took to keep him free. Jimbo hired a lawyer named Harry "Horserace" Harris to handle the case. Horserace was famous as much for his frequent trips to Arkansas to bet the races as for his brilliant courtroom defenses and his expensive legal fees. Horserace convinced the judge to drop the charges against Rango on grounds that the search of the car trunk was illegal; therefore, the evidence found in the trunk would not be admissible in court; therefore, there was no case.

To celebrate the occasion, the three friends spent all afternoon on the lake, skiing, drinking, and snorting cocaine. It was amazing how much water skiing Pam could do when she kept her nose packed with Peruvian flake.

Right before sundown they landed the boat, and Rango and Gary did some bank casting while Pam rode the elevator up to the house so she could start dinner. She had caught some nice bass that morning, and she planned to baste the fish in butter sauce while grilling them over a charcoal fire.

Rango tossed his lure next to a submerged log near the shoreline.

"You know, I think Jimbo likes having me owe him. He plans to make me work a lot of runs to pay off my legal fees."

"Beats going to jail."

"Yeah, but I'll never get rich unless I make one big score for Mr. Bodine."

Gary slowly reeled in his line.

"In fact, Jimbo's got a new project lined out, a project

he and I scouted out last year. He knows this fellow in Dallas who's hot to buy peyote buttons."

"Peyote buttons? I didn't know anybody still fooled with that stuff."

"This guy in Dallas is a chemist. He refines the buttons into mescaline. All I've got to do is drive down to south Texas, dig up the cactus, then drive the load up to Dallas."

"Sounds like a lot of exposure to me."

"Lots of profit, too," Rango added.

He reeled in his line and tossed it out again, this time a little farther from the shore. Seconds after the lure hit the water, Rango's reel zinged and his rod bent. He had hooked a big one.

The fish jumped and glittered in the twilight and hit the water with a loud splash. It jumped again, and Rango pulled hard on the line. Then the bass made a third leap, and Rango's line broke with a pop.

"Of all the lousy luck." Rango reeled in his broken line. "The good ones always escape."

Just then, Pam called down from the patio. "It's ready fellows."

Late that night, after Rango went home, Pam led Gary out onto the patio and they stood looking at the moon a while before riding the elevator down to the lake. When they reached the shore, Pam took off her shirt and jeans—she had stopped wearing underwear for the summer—and threw them on the grass. While Gary pulled off his clothes, Pam dived from the boat dock into the lake. The moonlight flashed on her skin as she splashed and swam. Then Gary jumped from the dock into the warm water.

Pam swam over to him and put her arms around his neck. Gary could feel her legs pumping to tread water, and her breasts brushed his chest. Then Pam left one arm around Gary's neck and helped him tread for a moment before reaching down and stroking his penis.

"Maybe we should get in shallow water." Gary fought to keep from going under.

"No. Not unless we have to."

Gary treaded water as hard as he could, but he knew he wouldn't be able to keep it up for long.

"Do it to me here, now."

Gary took a deep breath and went under water with Pam floating on top of him. He eased into her and tried to get his head up for a breath, but he couldn't find any air. For a moment, he thought Pam was holding him under; then he broke away and surfaced, gasping for breath.

Pam was treading water. She laughed.

"So much for mating at sea."

Pam turned and swam for the dock.

Gary followed her and they finished on dry land. Evolution suddenly made a lot of sense.

The next morning, Gary got the phone call from Jill McDaniel. He had almost forgotten about her, but the moment he heard her voice over the phone he remembered the good-looking brunette who drove the Cougar convertible.

"Gary, I realize that you don't trust me, but we have to have a meeting. I've got some news that directly affects Pam and you."

"How did you get this number? If you're still spying on us for Pam's father, forget it. We don't want anything to do with you or him."

"This has nothing to do with Dr. Jackson. It's nothing like that. It's a police matter, but I'd rather not explain it over the phone. Can we meet somewhere this afternoon?"

Gary thought about it for a moment. "Okay, at noon, under the Tower."

He didn't have any trouble spotting her on campus. Jill was sitting on the steps of the library-tower, and she was dressed in a black skirt and red silk blouse that set her apart from the students who wore cut-off jeans and tee-shirts. She waved to him when she saw Gary walking toward her, and because it was a warm sunny afternoon, they decided to have their talk right there on the steps of the library.

Gary was impressed with all the activity on the campus; there were students everywhere, most of them only a little younger than he, moving between classes. And for a moment as he sat on the steps and watched the girls walk by, Gary wondered why he didn't go back to school. Maybe it wasn't too late for him to find something to study. Maybe he and Pam could even attend classes together. After all, they had met in a class.

But Jill brought Gary's thoughts back to his here and now problems.

"I shouldn't be telling you this, but I've learned that you and Pam are on a bust list."

Gary looked at Jill a moment and wondered what she was up to.

"I thought you weren't a cop?"

"I'm not, but I have a close friend who is. After the La Grange sheriff sent out a report about Rango's coke bust, well, let's say that Travis County became more interested in his activities."

"Then you should know that Pam and I haven't done anything wrong."

Jill looked Gary in the eyes for a moment. She knew she was gambling and that Gary might catch her in a lie.

125

"Not recently, you mean."

Gary sat there and let his glance follow a pretty girl in short-shorts as she ran up the steps of the library.

"So what are you trying to say?"

"We need your help pinning down Jimbo Bodine. If you cooperate, we can make certain that you and Pam won't do jail time, won't even have records."

"Why are you so concerned about us?"

Jill shrugged.

"I'm not, really. It's only that I have a chance to help you and help my policeman friend, too. Besides, it's clear that you and Pam aren't in the same league as Jimbo."

"You know that Pam and I don't deal. And you know you're asking me to inform on a very dangerous guy. If Jimbo even suspected that I was trying to set him up, he'd kill me."

"Life is full of risks." Jill gave Gary her best poker face. "I'm trying to help you, as much because I made a bundle off of Pam's daddy as because of anything else."

Gary thought it over a moment. "I'm not agreeing with or admitting to anything. But what about Rango? Where does he fit into this deal?"

"That depends on how deeply involved he is in Jimbo's next run."

Jill was thankful that Gary had taken the bait.

Gary stood up and started down the steps.

"I'll think about it."

"Don't ponder it too long. You don't have that much time."

A few days later Gary and Rango loaded up Rango's pickup truck with fishing and camping gear, said good bye to Pam, and headed for Mexico. Gary told Pam that it was a fishing trip, and she promised to quit snorting cocaine for the few days that he would be away. They were getting good at lying to one another.

Gary had forgotten what a long, long drive it was from Austin to Starr County and Mexico. After they left the interstate at San Antonio and went south on highway 16, Texas seemed to inch by. They passed through Poteet, the "Strawberry Capital" of Texas, with its water tower painted to look like a giant strawberry, and continued south until the land became dry. When they reached Freer, Gary and Rango were deep in the heart of the Texas desert.

The sixty miles from Freer to Hebbronville were empty, quiet ones. Rango drove and Gary rode. The highway was the only sign of human influence; there were no gas stations, no houses, no ranch buildings or fences, only freedom as far as the eye could see. And there was plenty to see: mile after mile of open range covered with cactus and mesquite so tangled that cattle couldn't graze. But other, wilder creatures thrived. Rango spotted several mule deer, and once from the corner of his eye, Gary caught a quick blur of brown and the flash of a bobcat bounding into the brush.

It was late afternoon when they finally reached Roma. The Christmas decorations were still strung across the main street, the American flag drooped in front of the customs house, and the heat was enough to drive any Yankee out of Texas and into hell.

Rango parked the truck on the Texas side of the bridge and hid his joints and cocaine under the seat before he and Gary got out and started to walk across the border. The Rio Grande was running high and green.

"They must be releasing water from Lake Falcon," Rango said.

"Lots of land needs irrigation down here. Got to keep the bloom on the desert."

They crossed the bridge and stopped a moment to watch three Mexicans struggle with a huge pig. The sow was a monster, and the Mexicans had their hands full of trouble as they tried to shove the pig into the bed of an old pickup truck. She was still squealing when Rango and Gary ducked into a cafe for some late lunch of pork tacos.

"Let's party tonight." Rango used his shirtsleeve to wipe taco grease from his chin. "Tomorrow we'll spot the peyote."

The next morning, after they had nursed their hangovers with a breakfast of greasy huevos and had crossed over to Texas, Rango and Gary started the hunt. Peyote grew on the Mexican side of the border, too, but Rango had scouted out fields on the Texas side so they could avoid smuggling the buttons through customs.

Gary drove along the back roads of Starr County while Rango studied his topographical maps.

Several times they stopped, climbed over barbed wire fences, and walked far from the truck, searching under every clump of brush without finding a single peyote. Most of the time they were so close to the border that they could see Mexico, and Gary was worried about the Border Patrol spotting them. By late afternoon, Rango and Gary had only found two small fields of peyote, hardly enough to bother with.

"I'm sure about this next spot."

They climbed into the truck after another fruitless hike.

"That's what you've said about every place we've looked. Are you certain you and Jimbo checked this out last year?"

"Shit yes. Now get off my case. I know there's a big field somewhere in this stretch of road."

So they drove another few miles and parked the truck

again. They climbed a fence and walked about a mile from the road. Then Gary saw one large button growing in the open.

The peyote button was like an outpost stationed to guard a settlement; all down the rocky hillside stretched a huge stand of peyote.

"I told you so."

The field of buttons seemed endless; thousands and thousands of cacti glowed green in the sunlight. Waves of heat rippled off the field as if the buttons were radiating energy, and Gary could even smell the cacti baking in the afternoon sun.

"Amazing. There's a lot of money growing in this field."

"We should be careful when we harvest here," Gary said.

"Don't tell me that you believe in all that Mescalito bullshit."

"I believe in staying out of jail. That's the border over that way about three miles." Gary pointed to the south. "The federal boys are bound to patrol this area looking for wetbacks."

They hiked back to the truck and marked the way to the field by tying a bandanna to a fence post. Then they headed straight for Austin; Rango was in a big hurry to turn all those fleshy buttons into cocaine and folding money.

They were about thirty miles up 649, almost to highway 16, when they spotted the Mexican hitchhiking, and Rango pulled over to give the guy a lift. He looked about twenty years old, and he had illegal written all over him. He wore a pair of tattered pants and a dirty tee-shirt, and he smelled like the only bath he had gotten all year came when he swam the river. The fellow was nervous and worried looking as he climbed into the truck with his little canvas sack that held everything he owned.

The Mexican didn't speak any English, so Gary and Rango talked with him in Spanish. He was going to San Antonio where he had a brother who had promised to find him a job as a roofer, and he was plenty happy when Gary told him they'd take him all the way.

In Hebbronville, they stopped for lunch and the Mexican was embarrassed because he couldn't read the menu and didn't have any money for food. Gary said he would pay, and the Mexican ordered the only two things on the menu that were the same in both Spanish and English: hot cakes and coca-cola. The American dream, Gary thought as he watched the Mexican wolf down a tall stack of pancakes, is a powerful thing.

"God, that's cold water." Bob pulled himself out of the pool and hurried over to where Jill was sunning herself on the grassy hillside that bordered Barton Springs.

Even though the air temperature was nearly a hundred, the water flowing from the springs was icy cold. A lot of people were at the pool that day, most of them doing more sunbathing than swimming. Every now and then someone would dive into the water, cool down, then return to shore for more sun.

Bob toweled himself dry and looked at Jill. She was wearing a green one-piece suit

"Did I tell you I got accepted to law school?" Jill asked.

"No, you didn't mention it."

"Don't look so sad about it."

She put on a tee-shirt and then stared at the pool a moment. Jill had always considered Barton Springs, with its clear, cold water and its tall shade trees to be one of Austin's best spots.

"Why wouldn't it upset me some." Bob tried not to

sound too emotional. "You know the last thing I want is for you to leave town. After all, it took years for me to find you again."

"You don't need to worry yet. The only school that's agreed to take me is UT. I may study law right here in Austin if Harvard doesn't call soon."

Back at Jill's apartment, they watched the sailboats streak across the lake as the sun set behind the hills.

"You want some coffee?"

"I'll take a beer if you've got one."

Jill smiled and went off to the kitchen to fetch their drinks.

"You heard from our boy, you know, Gary?"

Jill handed him a cold Lone Star.

"Not since I last talked with him."

She reached into a jar and scooped some beans into the grinder. Then the grinder filled the kitchen with its noise for a moment, and soon the thick coffee aroma permeated the room.

"That's too bad. I was sure hoping to get a good tip out of him."

Jill poured herself a cup of dark, strong java.

"Gary said he'd think about our proposition. I got the feeling that he was scared enough to inform."

Out of habit Jill turned on the portable television that sat on the kitchen counter next to the stove. She recognized the voice on the commercial even before the picture had come to focus on the screen.

"That's him." The screen displayed the image of a gray-haired doctor dressed in a white jacket. "That's Pam's father, Doctor Jackson."

"He's a funny looking bird, isn't he?"

"Hush." Jill turned up the volume on the television set.

"I want to hear this."

"Where will it end?" The doctor gesticulated vividly for his television audience. "Ask yourselves that tonight. Ask yourself that question while you worry about little Johnnie or Susie and wonder where they are, what they're doing right now. You know they run with a bad crowd. They come home late. Their grades are falling. They seem distant and unapproachable. You know sometimes they've been drinking, and you suspect that they are involved with drugs. Maybe you've found some pills or a bag of marijuana. Maybe your son or daughter has come home late at night, too confused by LSD or speed to even speak with you. Where will it end? Ask yourself that."

The doctor paused a moment, looked straight into the camera, and jammed his hands into the pockets of his white coat. Then, in a softer, sadder tone, he went on.

"As a doctor, I can tell you where. Your child will be arrested, go crazy, or maybe even die from an overdose of dangerous drugs. That's where it will end, unless you do something, unless you take the action that will save your child's life."

Doctor Jackson paused a half moment this time.

"What can you do? I'll tell you what. First, you must realize that you're not alone, that all across this country a plague of drug abuse has spread to families like yours. We in the medical profession were slow to realize the magnitude of this problem, but now, professional help is here. Through our extensive sobriety treatment program at the Smarter Vista Clinics, your child can have a second chance at life, a chance to live and grow free of drugs. Give us a call at Smarter Vista for all the details. After all, isn't the life of your child worth a phone call?"

Doctor Jackson, his face frozen with sincerity and his hands still buried in his coat pockets, faded from the screen and a beer commercial came on the air.

"Jackson's a real salesman."

"Yeah, but he's got a point, I mean about the wave of drug abuse and all." Jill took a sip of coffee. "Have you seen Guadelupe Street lately? The entire campus looks like it's populated by refugees from the opium wars."

"I know. It was bad enough when there was a war on and all the crazy kids were determined to demonstrate their little hearts out. Now that their cause is gone, they just get doped up."

"I only wish we could get a little dirt on someone like Bodine."

Bob Maran sipped at his beer and thought a moment.

"Maybe you could give Gary another call. You know, remind him how bad it would look if Pam were arrested on a drug charge. I mean the founder of Smarter Vista sobriety centers would hate to have the world find out that his own daughter is a drug abuser."

"I doubt that Pam or Gary give a damn about the old man, but I'll see what I can do."

But the next morning it was Gary who telephoned Jill.

"There's a chance of a deal going down sometime pretty soon. Jimbo's in on it, but he's behind the scenes."

"That's all you have?"

"What more do you want? After all, I'm risking my life for you. What are you doing for me?"

"We're keeping you out of jail. That's what. I don't guess you saw Pam's father on television. He introducing his new drug treatment centers. It wouldn't look good if the doctor's daughter was busted on a drug charge, would it?"

Jill waited a moment for this to sink in. She looked out her apartment window at the storm clouds that were brewing in the western sky.

"I don't give a damn about him or his Smarter Vista. I only want Pam and me to be free, clear of all this mess. So I'm telling you, get ready. Something's going down and I'm only doing this one time. Next time I call, the show's on."

"But we've got to know a little in advance."

"I'll try, lady. I'll try."

V

"I think you've both lost your minds," Pam said. "Rango went to jail the last run he made. When will you two learn?"

"I've got to do it to pay back Bodine. And he told me he's going to send the buttons up to Dallas with a load of coke. We can buy some toot at wholesale prices then."

They were at the lake house, sitting at the kitchen table, drinking coffee.

"What about that fellow Buck? You know, the guy with the big old Ford?" Gary asked. "Do you think we could get him to drive?"

"I bet we could get at least four hundred pounds of peyote in the trunk of his car."

"All you two are going to get is trouble."

They found Buck the next evening; he was working as a deejay at a tits and ass bar called the Doll House. A skinny girl with big breasts was doing her shake-it act when Rango and Gary walked in. The place was packed with people and the air was clouded with cigarette smoke. The marks—mostly cowboys and frat rats—lined the low stage waiting to slip a dollar bill under the dancer's g-string.

Rango explained the plan to Buck.

"I don't know fellows. It sounds pretty dangerous to me."

"You'll get a third of the buttons. All you have to do is drive. You're a driver, aren't you?"

Buck put "Walk This Way" by a new band called Aereosmith on the sound system, and another girl went on display.

Gary couldn't help but stare at her naked breasts and wonder how many of the girls split their take with Buck.

"Okay," Buck finally said. "I'll do it. When do we leave?"

"Friday sound okay with you?"

"Sure." Buck sorted through his record albums. "Friday morning."

Rango and Buck arrived at the lake house early Friday morning in Buck's old Ford. Gary said good-bye to Pam—she'd been staying drunk to avoid the post-cocaine depression—and he climbed into the back seat of the old car.

Rango had everything ready; the car was loaded with food, an ice chest full of beer, some fishing gear, and a tackle box. They would be another bunch of guys on a weekend fishing trip except that they carried hoes and burlap bags in the trunk of the old Ford.

Buck was a good driver, and when they hit the vacant stretch of flat desert between Freer and Hebbronville, he pushed the car up to a hundred miles an hour. The desert passed by in a blur of brown; the lines on the highway didn't seem to have any spaces between them.

"Better slow her up."

It made Gary nervous to go that fast, especially since Buck was steering with one hand and holding a beer in the other.

"I got this Ford tuned to a hum and we got the whole highway to ourselves. Fuck fifty-five."

Buck took a swig of beer and stomped the gas pedal to the floor. They were going about a hundred and ten. Finally he slowed down to ninety. They covered the twenty miles of blacktop from Hebbronville to Randado in ten minutes and then shot down highway 649 to Roma and Falcon State Park.

Falcon Lake always seemed out of place to Gary; it was a fresh water sea located in the middle of North America's largest desert. They pitched Rango's tent on the dirty shore of the state park camping area before they took a walk. The place was crowded with people and travel trailers. The old folks hung around their R.V.s and sipped beer while the kids played in the dirt or chased roadrunners up and down the sand trails. Buck got a bass lure from the tackle box, rigged up a rod and reel, and went fishing. Rango and Gary crawled into the tent and smoked a joint. Rango was jumpy, and sweat had caused his blue cowboy shirt to change to a darker shade.

"This is going to be a good run, amigo, and after this one all I have to do is a run with Jimbo's coke and I'll be out of debt and in the money."

"I think you'd quit dealing."

"Why?" Rango gave Gary a puzzled look.

"I got a feeling, you know. A feeling that's it's time to lay low a while."

Rango passed the joint to Gary.

"You were always too paranoid to be in this business."

The pink sunrise found them barreling along the dusty back road toward the peyote field. The bandanna was still tied to the fence line where Rango had put it, and it only took a moment to unload the gear from the trunk of the old Ford. Gary tossed the hoes and sacks and the canteen of water over the fence while Rango gave Buck his final instructions.

"Meet us here at two sharp. That's plenty of time."

"I'll see you then."

Buck sped away, kicking up gravel and dust.

Rango and Gary hurried over the fence and into the thick brush. It was hot, and the walk back to the field was longer than Gary remembered. Then they were there on the hillside, looking at the seemingly endless patch of peyote. Many of the buttons were growing in clumps beneath mesquites or prickly pears, protected by shade and thorns.

Rango took a hoe and started harvesting the cactus. Soon he and Gary had filled a burlap bag with the buttons.

"You keep picking. I'll carry this one to the road."

Rango shouldered the sack.

"I'll have another one ready by the time you get back."

Rango nodded and started walking toward the road with the big sack over his shoulder. There was no way of knowing for certain, but Gary guessed that the bag weighed at least fifty pounds. His hands were crisscrossed with scratches and his back was beginning to ache, but Gary kept digging up the buttons.

After Rango had carried three sacks to the highway, he and Gary took a break. They crowded into a spot of shade created by a large stand of mesquite and drank most of a canteen full of water. They were both soaked in sweat. Suddenly an armadillo bounded out of the brush, froze when it spotted Rango, then leapt back into the cover.

"Guess we had better get with it. Time is money and all that."

"Why don't we switch jobs for a while," Gary suggested.

"Sure. You can carry this bag back."

Gary lifted the bag of buttons to his shoulder.

"Must weigh sixty pounds."

"Then that sack's worth about two thousand dollars."

Rango bent down and started chopping at a clump of peyote as Gary turned toward the highway. He had only gone about twenty yards when he heard Rango yell. Gary dropped the sack of buttons and ran back to where Rango was standing. He was holding the hoe like a weapon, and Gary heard the buzz of a snake's rattle before he saw the diamond-back. The snake was at least five feet long and was coiled up a few yards in front of Rango.

Then Rango came down hard with the hoe, striking the snake twice before severing its head with the second blow.

"Bastard almost got me."

Rango held down the snake's writhing body with one boot and cut the rattle off the snake's tail with the blade of the hoe. When he stepped away from the diamond-back, the rattler coiled and flipped in the sand as if it were still alive.

Gary was headed back to the fence with the eighth sack of peyote when he heard the faint sound of an engine. He hit the ground and crawled under a patch of mesquite as the plane zoomed over his hiding place with a flash of blue and white. It was flying so low that Gary could see the INS emblem painted on its side. The plane circled and then disappeared over the horizon. Gary carried the sack to the highway and hid it with the others under a bunch of mesquite branches before hurrying back to Rango to see if he had been spotted.

"I don't think they saw me." Rango pointed to a shallow gully that bordered the field. "I was down there when I heard them coming. But we'd better get moving anyway. It's about time to finish up."

They each filled one more sack and started for the road. When they reached the fence, they uncovered the sacks and sized up the loot. There were ten bags, and Gary figured that each weighed about fifty pounds. Five hundred pounds meant nearly twenty thousand dollars. Not too bad, Gary thought, not for two days work, and he wondered if he could figure out a way to get paid before Jimbo got busted for the load. Rango covered the bags with the mesquite branches, and he and Gary waited for Buck to arrive.

They waited and waited and waited and waited. Two hours later, Rango spotted a swirl of dust moving along the road. It was Buck, speeding down the dirt road at about seventy miles per hour. He was going so fast that he missed Rango and Gary and sped past, stopping and backing up only when Rango jumped onto the road and waved.

Buck got out of the car, but he left the engine running.

"Where the hell have you been? We had a INS plane buzzing us out there. What if they'd sent a patrol down this road?"

"The damn car broke down. I stopped and it wouldn't start up. Thought for a while that I'd killed the battery, but it finally turned over."

"Let's get going. We'll be lots safer when we hit the paved highway."

Gary wondered if Jill McDaniel and her cop friend would help him if he got busted before they could set up Jimbo Bodine. They probably wouldn't bother, Gary decided. Besides, it would be safer for him to serve time than to let Jimbo know about the double cross.

Rango stuffed the bags of peyote into the trunk and covered everything with blankets. It was a tight fit and the old car rode low because of all the weight.

At last they were on highway 649, heading north at a careful fifty-five miles per hour. Gary figured they would probably make it back to Austin all right, and he started to relax a little. They passed a sign that announced a roadside park, and Rango wanted to stop.

"Come on, man," Buck said. "We got all this dope on us and you want to stop?"

"I got to piss. You want me to do it in the car?"

Buck pulled into the park and stopped the car under one of the few trees in that part of Texas. There were three tables on the small picnic ground. The state must have watered the grass often because it was green and lush.

"Make it quick. I'm afraid to cut the engine."

Rango scaled the fence that separated the picnic area from the desert. On his way back he stopped to read the sign the highway department had posted on the fence. The sign said:

BEWARE OF POISONOUS REPTILES

Rango took out his pocketknife and unhinged the plaque.

Rango got back into the car.

"That's the kind of shit that got you arrested in La Grange," Gary said. "You're asking for another bust."

"Lighten up, amigo. That sign will look great hanging in the living room next to my rattle."

Rango took the snake's rattle out of his pocket and showed it to Buck.

"Put that sign over your water bed, man," Buck said. "That way the chicks will have some idea who they're dealing with."

It was late afternoon when they pulled into Hebbron-ville. Gary was beginning to feel at home in the little town. The heat was bouncing off the pavement in wide waves as they drove past the courthouse and the town square.

"We got to stop for gas. If the car won't start up, at least we'll be at a station."

Buck stopped and filled the Ford up with gas. The car started on the first try, and since they had skipped lunch and the car seemed to be working, they decided to get something to eat.

They had a choice of restaurants, the Dairy Queen or the little cafe called the Texan where Rango and Gary had bought the hot cakes for the wetback. They decided on the Texan because they could get beer there. The Texan had a row of booths against one wall and a long lunch counter where some locals were sipping at their brews. A deputy sheriff was talking on the pay phone, but he didn't have any reason to notice Rango and Buck and Gary; they looked like all the other cowboys. After a chicken-fried steak and a couple of beers, Gary was feeling pretty good. He mentally clicked off the towns ahead: Freer, Poteet, San Antonio, San Marcos, and finally Austin. But Hebbronville is a long way from Austin, and that fact was driven home when Buck turned the key in the old car and nothing happened, nothing except the buzz of the battery trying to juice the engine.

"Same thing as this morning."

They got out of the car and Buck lifted the hood. All the connections seemed okay.

"You boys got problems?"

The deputy who had been on the phone walked up and peered under the hood. He was a young Chicano with a neatly trimmed mustache, and he took off his dark sunglasses so he could get a better look at the Ford's motor.

"Come on, then," the deputy said. "I'll help you push start her."

Buck got behind the wheel, and Rango, Gary, and the deputy pointed the car down the empty side street next to the Texan. They pushed, and pushed, and pushed; but every time Buck popped the clutch, the car froze and the tires grabbed gravel.

"You got some serious trouble, here." The policeman mopped the sweat from his forehead with his handkerchief. "Where you boys from, anyhow?"

"Austin," Rango said.

"We've been down at Falcon," Gary added. "Hasn't been our lucky trip. Fished all yesterday and didn't get a thing, and now this happens."

"Well, I'll bring the patrol car around and push you up the street to Ramirez's place. He's the best mechanic in town."

The deputy pulled his black and white around from the cafe and eased up to the Ford's back bumper. Gary kept thinking that the trunk was bound to pop open. The cop pushed Buck's Ford back across the highway and about five blocks up another side street, stopping in front of a clapboard house with an adjacent garage. Buck went and knocked on the front door of the house while Rango and Gary shook hands with the cop, thanking him and sighing with relief when he finally drove away.

"Can't say exactly what it is," Ramirez said.

He was a thin old fellow with gray hair.

"Could even be the pistons."

"How long to fix it?"

"I couldn't get started on a job like this until tomorrow. I'll have to break into the engine, looks like. Might cost a bit, too, if I have to do that."

Rango and Gary and Buck looked at one another for a moment.

"We need to be at work in the morning," Buck said. "How about I leave it here and let you see what's wrong. Then I'll call you tomorrow evening and you can tell me how much it'll take to fix?"

"Sounds okay." Ramirez wiped his hands on a shop rag.

They left the car parked behind Ramirez's house and walked back to the Texan, where they took a booth and ordered a round of beers.

"We got to do something," Buck said. "There's no way we're going to leave this town with that load still in the trunk of my car."

"We understand." Rango took a long swig of beer. "We're not going to lose the car or the load."

"We'll have to call Austin," Gary said. "We got to try to find somebody who'll come for us."

"I'll try Jimbo."

Rango got up and headed for the pay phone. He made several calls, then came back to the booth.

"Jimbo didn't answer. And nobody else wants to come down here."

Buck tried his friends next, but nobody was willing to drive five hundred round-trip miles to pull a safari of stranded peyote hunters back to civilization.

"There's one person we didn't try," Rango said. "And I think Gary should call her."

"Pam will be too drunk to drive down here. But I'll give it a try anyway."

Gary went to the pay phone and dialed the lake house. After about ten rings, Pam answered the phone.

"We've run into some trouble down here, and we need you to come and help us out."

"Where are you?"

"Hebbronville."

"That's a long way."

"Come on down and pick us up, please."

"I told you I didn't want to do anything like that. I told you, didn't I?"

For a moment Gary thought about telling Pam the

143

whole story, that he had to run the peyote deal to set Jimbo up for the cops. But he knew he would never be able to make Pam understand. She was so messed up anymore that Gary doubted that she understood anything.

"Look, if you give a damn about me, you'll get in the car and come down here. We'll be waiting for you in front of the Texan Cafe. It's right on the highway. You won't be able to miss it in this little town."

Pam didn't say anything for a moment, then she finally gave in.

"Okay"

"Good girl. When will you leave?"

"I can start in thirty minutes."

"Okay, darling. Hurry. We'll be waiting."

Gary hung up the phone and walked back to the booth.

"Well, is she coming?"

"She's coming, but she was bitchy about it."

They waited inside the Texan until ten o'clock, when the restaurant closed. Buck went back to the car, hoping to catch some sleep. Rango and Gary settled down under the Trailways bus sign in front of the cafe and waited for Pam.

The town's two traffic lights swung in the dry breeze, blinking out their yellow caution signals. Gary and Rango had a good view of the Hebbronville town square, and they could see the deputies go in and out of the courthouse and the jail. About midnight, a patrol car eased into the restaurant parking lot.

"You fellows waiting for the bus?"

He was an older cop with a tired, doing-my-job look on his face.

"No. We had car trouble. A friend is coming to pick us up."

"Let's see some ID."

Rango and Gary fumbled a moment and handed over

their driver's licenses.

The policeman handed the licenses back.

"Where's the car now?"

"Down the street at Ramirez's shop," Gary said. "One of your deputies helped us push it over there this afternoon."

"Leaving it here, then?"

"Don't have much choice. We've got to be back at work tomorrow."

"Okay." The policeman gave Rango a long look. "Making sure, is all."

He started up his patrol car and drove off. Rango let out a sigh.

"God help us."

"Settle down. Pam will be here in a couple of hours."

It was nearly one in the morning when Pam arrived driving the Mustang.

"Christ," Gary said. "I thought you'd never get here."

"This place is almost all the way to Mexico. It takes a long time to drive to Mexico from Austin."

Her face was pinched and angry. She had tucked her hair into a sailor's cap, and she was wearing jeans and a green army shirt with sergeant's strips on the shoulders. Since the war had ended, used military clothing had become the rage on campus.

Rango and Gary got into the Mustang and they drove up the street to where Buck was sleeping in the car. They woke him and started shifting bags of peyote from the old Ford to the new Mustang. Rango grabbed a bag, caught it on the trunk latch, and tore the sack, sending peyote buttons bouncing everywhere.

"Damn."

"Get them all," Buck said. "I don't want them finding any around my car tomorrow."

Buck flicked on the taillights, and Rango and Gary

gathered up as many buttons as they could find. They could only get six of the ten sacks in the Mustang's trunk, so they put the other sacks in the back seat and threw a blanket over them.

"Okay," Pam said. "I need to get some gas and then we'll be set."

"You're out of gas?" Gary knew that there wasn't going to be a station open in Hebbronville at two in the morning.

"Well, it was full when I left Austin. I stopped in Freer, but all the stations were closed."

"That wasn't real bright," Rango put in. "You should have gassed up in San Antonio. There's not much in these hick-shit towns down here."

"I'm not very smart. I should have stayed in Austin and let you rot."

"There's gas in my car," Buck said. "We could siphon some into the Mustang."

But they couldn't find anything to siphon with.

"Come on," Rango said. "I got an idea, but you have to keep watch for me."

Gary and Rango wandered off through the back streets of Hebbronville. The roads were unpaved and most of the homes they passed were shacks or old mobile homes. Finally Rango saw what he was looking for in a yard without a dog.

"Give me some warning if you see anyone."

Rango slipped over the picket fence.   The yard was dark, and there were no lights on inside the house. He crawled across the lawn and up to the side of the house where a garden hose was attached to a faucet. He took out his pocket knife and cut off a three-foot long section of hose; then he crawled back to the fence where Gary was waiting.

"That'll do the trick." Rango waved the hose through

the air.

But when they got back to the cars, they discovered that the gas tank on Buck's old Ford was more than a foot lower than the cap on the Mustang's tank. No matter how hard Rango sucked and spit, he couldn't get the gas to flow the distance.

"What now, bright boy?" Pam asked.

Buck found a sixteen-ounce Coke bottle on the ground.

"We could fill this and then pour it into the Mustang."

"That'll take forever." Pam gagged at the notion of using gasoline for a mouthwash. "I'll go stand on the corner and keep watch in case anyone comes up this way."

Buck, Rango, and Gary took turns sucking the hose, filling the Coke bottle, and pouring the gas into the Mustang's tank. Rango swallowed some gasoline and threw up on his boots.

They put eighty Coke bottles full of gas into the Mustang and started out, hoping to make the hundred and thirty miles to San Antonio. The ride back was a relief even though Gary and Rango had to sit on the sacks of peyote, and the smell of the puke on Rango's boots filled the car. Finally, Buck produced a joint of Colombian redbud that mellowed them to the road. Pam drove north at a fifty-five mile per hour crawl, stopping in San Antonio for gas and arriving in Austin in time for the morning traffic jam. And as they sat in the morning gridlock on I-35, Gary wished that his nightmare were over and that he too was another normal person heading for his boring nine-to-five job.

VI

The next morning was fine and sunny, and Pam and Gary took breakfast on the patio of their lake house. Gary buttered a piece of wheat toast, and Pam sipped at her coffee and looked out at the lake. A boat was pulling a skier across the smooth water, and the faint hum of the boat's motor echoed off the hills. They could smell the peyote even though Gary had wrapped the buttons in plastic bags and hidden them in the back bedroom.

"I'm going to Dallas with Rango," Pam said. "I've been thinking about my father. He and I need to talk things over away from any distractions."

"So I've become a distraction?" Gary stared at the motor boat as it cut a wake across the lake.

"That's not what I meant. I want to try and work some things out with my dad, is all."

"Guess you'll do what you want."

"What I want is to catch a ride with Rango when he goes up to Dallas."

Pam poured herself another cup of coffee and spooned in two scoops of sugar. For a while she and Gary sat there, looking out at the lake and the hills.

"Are you fucking him again?"

"Jesus, you'll never let me forget that, will you?"

So Gary shut up and hoped for the best when Pam and Rango left for Dallas.

A few days later, someone rang the doorbell. When Gary opened the door, Jimbo Bodine and one of his cowboys stormed into the room. The moment they were inside, Jimbo's man pulled his pistol.

"You should have run, too, you poor bastard," Jimbo said.

"What the hell are you talking about?"

Jimbo looked around the house while his man held Gary at gunpoint. Jimbo's helper wore a suit and tie and cowboy boots; he was a tall, heavy-set fellow with a nose that looked like it had been broken more than once.

"You punks really thought that you could pull a fast one on old Jimbo, didn't you. After all the work I gave you. Amigo, you were dead wrong. Now where's that son of a bitch Rango, and what's he done with my cocaine?"

Jimbo nodded to the man with the broken nose. Before Gary could duck, the cowboy popped him in the face with the pistol. Gary went down bleeding.

"You'd better stop stalling and tell me where Rango is."

"I swear I don't know." Gary spat out a tooth. "They said they were going to Dallas."

Gary felt of his jaw and swallowed some blood.

"If that's the way you want it."

Jimbo's man pulled Gary to his feet. Jimbo took a cigar out of his pocket; he lit the cigar and puffed until it burned red hot at its end.

"Come on boy. You'd better tell me where Rango is. He was supposed to deliver a pound of my coke to a fellow in Fort Worth after he sold the peyote. The peyote deal went okay, but that was the last anyone saw of Rango."

"They took the peyote and went to Dallas. That's all I know."

Jimbo ripped open Gary's shirt and pressed the cigar to Gary's left nipple. Gary screamed. He could smell his own flesh burning.

"You've got to believe me." Gary gasped with pain.

"Why are you covering for Rango?" Jimbo waved the cigar around Gary's face. "All he ever did for you was fuck your chick. He used to tell me all about what a tiger she was in the sack. Said she knew a thousand and one positions."

"I'm telling you the truth. I swear."

Jimbo nodded again, and his man let go of Gary and pushed him to the floor before placing the gun barrel to the back of Gary's head. Gary shivered. He closed his eyes and prayed.

"Okay, Zero," Jimbo said. "It's all right. Let him be."

The cowboy with the nose stepped back and away. Gary could still feel the pressure at the back of his head from where the gun had been.

Jimbo went into the bedroom and found the phone. He unscrewed the mouthpiece, inserted a thin silver disk, and made a call. When Jimbo came back into the living room, Gary was sitting on the couch inspecting his burn.

"You want I should hurt him some more?" Zero asked.

"No. Let him save some face. He might need it later."

Zero laughed.

"And you'd better be telling me the truth because when I find that fucker Rango I'm going to hurt him bad, and if you've been shitting me, I'll kill your ass, too."

"What happened to you?" Jill McDaniel asked.

She and Gary were on campus, sitting in lobby of the student center. It was late afternoon of a summer school session, and there weren't many students milling around. The right side of Gary's face was swollen and bruised a deep purple, and Jill noticed that he moved his left arm stiffly, as if something were the matter with his chest.

"Mr. Bodine and one of his thugs came to visit me the other night."

"Why didn't you call? We've been waiting."

Gary stared at Jill a moment and wished that he had never met her.

"Look lady, I called you here because the deal is off. Rango and Pam have run off together, and Jimbo almost killed me the other night. Now if you want to have me arrested, fine. If not, then leave me alone because there's no way I'm messing with Jimbo Bodine again."

With that Gary got up, looked at Jill McDaniel one last time, then walked out of the building.

When he saw Gary leave, Bob Maran hung up the phone he had been pretending to use, left the phone booth, and went over to where Jill was sitting.

"What's the latest news from the world of crime?" Bob took the chair Gary had left. "Our boy looked pretty beat up."

"He claims he had a run in with Jimbo. Says he won't work for us. Besides, according to Gary, the gang's broken up. He said something about the girl going off with Rango."

Bob Maran took off his Stetson hat and ran his fingers through his thick, black hair. A television was blaring away from the opposite side of the lobby. The program was a rerun of *Dr. Bill's Medicine Show*, but nobody was watching.

"Looks like we've wasted a lot of time with these people."

"Unless he's trying to throw us off track," Jill said. "But if Bodine knew that Gary had turned informer, he wouldn't have beat up Gary. He would have killed him."

"Maybe. And besides, who could have told Bodine that Gary was informing? It doesn't add up."

They sat silently, thinking through the possibilities.

"Gary claimed that Rango and Pam had run off together. Rango has something Bodine wants back. Might be the girl, or maybe it's dope."

Bob put his hat on and got up from his chair.

"Come on." He took her by the hand. "I got a feeling Jimbo Bodine might be staking our boy out. This case may not be over yet."

As he walked across campus and eyed the students who looked so carefree and happy, Gary cussed himself for not being one of them. He would try harder this time, he decided, try harder to steer clear of trouble. He would save money and use what was left of his inheritance to go back to college. He would work; he would study; he would build some sort of future for himself.

He headed straight to Chris' Liquor Store and asked Chris for his old job back. The Greek took one look at Gary's bruised face and hired him to work that very afternoon.

"I knew you were in trouble when you started hanging out with that fancy-pants cowboy." Chris watched as Gary stocked the beer cooler. "What's his name, Rango?"

"His real name's Ralph."

"And now look what happened to you."

"Things got a little crazy, that's all."

Gary opened a case of Pearl beer and started shoving six-packs onto the cooler racks. It felt good to be back at work, back in the cooler, breathing frosty air and shivering with cold while the rest of Texas sweated in the heat.

"You thought you could beat the system. Get rich quick, hey?"

Gary looked at Chris. He was still fat and happy.

"I screwed up, is all. It's no big deal now."

Chris took a big can of beer from a case, opened the can, and took a sip of the cold brew. He didn't usually drink in the liquor store because it was against the law.

"You think it was easy for me when I first came to America?" Chris took another sip. "This is a wonderful land, this America. Here I work all the time, it's true, but I have four stores and some fine sons to give them to. In Greece, I worked all the time and never had a damn thing. Here there is a chance, at least. Go back to school. Save your pay. Things will work out."

When Gary finally made it back to the lake house that night, he was exhausted. His jaw was bothering him, and he was jumpy. On the way home from the liquor store, he thought he saw someone following him; headlights in the rearview had seemed to trace his every turn. Finally he decided that he was only being paranoid.

He had poured a drink and was about to relax a while on the patio when the phone rang.

It was Pam, and she was crying so hard that at first Gary couldn't understand what she was saying. Finally she calmed down to a mild sobbing.

"Gary, you've got to come and help me."

"Why did you do it, baby? Why did you go like that?"

"He made me. He keeps me locked up. Won't let me out of the house. He even cuffs me to the bed when he leaves. I won't get another chance to call. He's so stoned that he forgot to move the phone when he left."

"Why should I believe that? You wanted to ride to Dallas with Rango."

"Please, you got to help me, please."

Gary listened a moment while Pam cried into the phone.

"Okay. Tell me where you are."

"We're in San Antonio. It's a trailer park. The address is 1213 Adobe."

"Where's Rango now?"

"He said he was going for beer. Please hurry."

"Listen to me. I'll be there late tonight, after Rango's asleep. You be ready to go, hear?"

"Rango never sleeps anymore. He does coke all the time. He's gone crazy."

Pam cried into the phone some more, then said, "God, he's back."

The line went dead and Gary hung up the phone. He said, "1213 Adobe, 1213 Adobe," over and over again until he had memorized the address. Even though he wasn't certain he could believe Pam, he could forgive her. It was Rango he wanted to settle with, and he would have walked to San Antonio for a shot at him. Gary went to the bedroom and got his .38 Smith and Wesson revolver, the one that had belonged to his father, from under the mattress. He stuck the pistol in his belt.

When he stepped out of the front door of the lake house, Gary was met by Jimbo's man, Zero.

"Turn around and go back inside."

Bob Maran put the binoculars down in his lap and gave Jill a nudge. She had been asleep for more than an hour, and Bob had to nudge her again to wake her.

"Come on, sleepy head. We've got some action going down."

Jill blinked and yawned and sat straight up in the passenger's seat of Bob's unmarked Chevy Impala.

"So what's happening?"

"I'm not certain."

Bob put the binoculars to his eyes and focused on the front door of the lake house. He had pulled the car behind a stand of trees that edged the road about a quarter mile down from Gary's house. They were waiting for Gary when he returned from the liquor store, and Bob had been about to call it a night when a car had stopped in front of the lake house.

"A big, tall guy got out of that car and went inside. Wasn't anybody I'd seen before from what I could tell."

A Ford LTD came down the road and passed by Jill and Bob before turning into the drive at Gary's house. This time Bob recognized the man who got out; it was Jimbo Bodine.

"Looks like the stakeout was a good idea," Pam said.

"Yeah, but there's three of them, if you count Gary."

He took his service revolver out of its holster and

opened the cylinder to check the load. Then he snapped the cylinder shut and holstered the gun. The police radio crackled.

"Shouldn't we call for some back up?"

"Let's hold off on that. They may lead us to the stash."

"He was carrying this when he went out." Zero showed Gary's revolver to Jimbo.

"Mr. Tough Guy, aren't you?" Jimbo took the weapon and stuck it in his belt.

"What do you want?"

"Oh man." Zero rubbed his broken nose. "You're a real joker."

"We've been keeping a close watch on you," Jimbo said. "Where you fixing to go?"

Gary looked surprised. He wondered how Jimbo knew he was about to leave the house.

"Yeah, we know where you were headed. Jimbo wired your phone last time we were here. We've been picking up all your calls."

"What were you going to do with this." Jimbo patted the revolver in his belt.

"I was going after Rango."

Jimbo laughed, went into the bedroom, and removed the silver disk from the phone. He returned and tossed the disk to Zero.

"You know something, boy? This turned out pretty good for you. I believe that you were telling me the truth. I may not have to kill you after all."

"So what happens next?"

Gary was beaten and he knew it. Jimbo was smarter, and better equipped, than he had suspected.

"You told Pam you'd be there late tonight. So I figure we ought to head down there and pay them a little visit."

Jimbo nodded to Zero and they shoved Gary out of the house and into Jimbo's LTD. Zero drove while Jimbo and Gary sat in the back seat. Jimbo pulled the revolver from his belt and held it in his lap. They drove past Bob Maran's Chevy, but all they noticed was a couple necking in the front seat.

Soon they were in Austin, heading south on I-35 toward San Antonio.

"I knew sooner or later they would call you," Jimbo said. "That's why I planted the bug the day we roughed you up."

"What's going to happen to Pam?" Gary looked out the car window.

"Forget that slut. You'd better worry about you."

"I wasn't able to get the license plate, were you?"

"No," Jill stared ahead into the night.

They were speeding down I-35 at about eighty miles an hour, trying to catch up with Jimbo's car.

"I shouldn't of let him get so much distance on me back there. But I was afraid they'd spot us."

"I saw them turn south on 35. I bet they headed for San Antonio."

"I'll catch up with him." Bob pressed the gas pedal and the Impala jumped to ninety miles per hour. "But I guess I'd better radio DPS and the San Antonio police anyway, let them know something is going down."

Bob picked up the microphone and cleared the radio for a call.

It was midnight when Zero drove them across loop 410 and headed straight through downtown San Antonio on 35. The freeway wasn't crowded at that hour, and as they swung around town, Gary watched the aircraft warning lights blink on and off atop the Tower of the Americas. From 35, Zero took them west, heading toward Kelly airfield. Jimbo checked the address on a city map.

"Take the next exit."

They swung off the freeway and onto the access road. Gary wasn't exactly sure where they were, only that they were somewhere on the southwest side of San Antonio. Jimbo kept his eyes on the street signs.

"How come they call you Zero?" Gary asked.

"Zero bars are my favorite type of candy."

"Turn left on the next corner," Jimbo told his man. "And you keep quiet."

They turned and went a few more blocks before Jimbo ordered Zero to turn again, this time into a trailer park. As they drove through the park, past hundreds and hundreds of trailers that lined dozens of twisting streets, Gary realized that the park was actually a mobile-home suburb, almost as large as a small town. There were few street lights, and Zero had to dodge an overturned trash can that had blown onto the road.

Finally Jimbo found Adobe Street, and then he spotted his van parked in front of one of an old Airstream trailer.

"That's it. I'd know my van anywhere."

Zero continued down the street and parked the LTD. They were only three trailers down from the Airstream.

"Okay, let's make it quick and quiet. We'll go through the back door, do it, grab the coke and go."

Zero grunted his agreement and screwed a six inch silencer onto the barrel of the flat automatic pistol he took from his belt. Jimbo waved the .38 revolver under Gary's nose.

"And you keep your mouth shut if you want to live. I'll be right behind you."

They got out of the LTD and walked across a patch of

grass that was someone's backyard. There were only a few lights on in the trailers around them, but the hum of air conditioners filled the hot night. When they got to the Airstream, Gary started to say something, but Jimbo clamped his hand over Gary's mouth and nudged him in the back with the pistol.

Jimbo nodded and Zero went up the steps to the door and turned the handle to test the lock. Jimbo tightened his grip over Gary's mouth and jerked back Gary's head.

"Okay," Jimbo whispered, "do it."

Zero dropped his left shoulder low like a football player making a block and rammed the door. The lock snapped and Zero rushed into the trailer. Pam screamed and there was a thud-thud-thud of silenced shots. Gary started inside the trailer, but Jimbo hit him with the pistol and sent him to his knees.

Zero flicked on a light.

"It's over."

Jimbo kicked Gary into the trailer, holding the .38 on him all the while.

The first thing Gary saw was Pam. She lay on the bed, naked against the white sheets. There was a small, red hole between her breasts and a large stain of blood on the sheets. Gary rushed over and knelt beside her.

Pam's eyes fluttered.

"I'm sorry," she said.

Then she moaned. Gary stood up and looked at her. Pam's cold blue eyes seemed to stare at him, but she was gone.

"Was he waiting for us?"

"He went for his shotgun, but he never had a chance."

Zero pointed to Rango. He was face down on the floor with a double barrel sawed-off shotgun next to him.

Jimbo started searching the trailer for the cocaine

Rango had taken. He found it in a suitcase hidden in the bathroom. Inside the suitcase were stacks of hundred dollar bills and four bags of coke. Jimbo thumbed though the bills and held a bag of coke in his hand, estimating the weight.

"Looks like he sold most of the coke. But there's plenty of money here."

Rango moaned.

"Watch out. He's still alive."

"Not for long," Zero said.

He went over to Rango and put the pistol to Rango's temple.

"Wait."

Gary looked at Pam. She stared back at him with her dead eyes. All he could think was that if she hadn't called him, she would still be alive.

Jimbo and Zero lifted Rango into a chair. Rango's shirt was soaked with blood; he had been gut shot, and he moaned again when they moved him.

"Get his pants off," Jimbo said. "Hurry."

They pulled off Rango's jeans, and Gary watched as Jimbo and Zero dragged Rango across the trailer to the bathroom. They sat him down on the toilet and propped him up with his elbows on his knees. Then Jimbo took a knife from his pocket, switched open the blade, and cut off Rango's penis. Rango screamed and blood spurted out of him like pee. Then he fell to the floor. Zero lifted Rango back up on the toilet, and Jimbo struck the bloody penis between Rango's lips as if it were a lit cigar.

"Bet he's been wanting to do that all his life," Zero said.

Gary moved across the room to where the shotgun was lying on the floor. He picked up the gun and leveled it at Jimbo and Zero. Gary cocked back both hammers; Jimbo and his man turned around. Gary pulled both triggers. The trailer shook with noise. Blood and bits of flesh splattered the bathroom.

Then everything was quiet except for the ringing in Gary's ears. Jimbo had been blown up against the toilet, pinning Rango to his throne. Zero lay on the bathroom floor, face down in his own blood.

On the nightstand next to Pam's body, Gary found the keys to the van that was parked in front of the trailer. Gary brushed back Pam's hair, closed her eyes, and pulled a sheet over her.

Then he picked up the briefcase, ran out of the trailer, and got into the van; he started the engine and drove away.

As he sped onto the freeway, two squad cars with their lights flashing raced by him, heading for the trailer park. Gary drove west until he hit the loop, and then he turned south on highway 16, headed for Freer, Hebbronville, Roma and the border.

"Damn it. I know I saw them turn in here."

All the streets and all the mobile homes seemed to look the same in the poorly-lit park.

"Maybe they went that way." Jill nodded toward yet another dark street lined with trailers.

"Maybe so."

Bob turned and began driving up and down the sinuous streets, searching all the while for the LTD.

"There it is." Jill pointed to the LTD that was parked along the curb.

"Guess we'd better have a look around." Bob pulled over and parked the car.

When Jill and Bob approached the LTD, two police cars came speeding down the street. The squad cars stopped three trailers from where Bob had parked his car, and four officers with their pistols drawn scrambled out.

One of the policemen spotted Bob and Jill standing in the street. He leveled his pistol at them and shouted, "Hands in the air, now."

Both Jill and Bob immediately obeyed and in seconds another officer was on them, patting them down for weapons.

"I'm a Travis County Constable. I'm wearing my service revolver, and my badge is in my wallet."

It took only a moment for the police to take Bob's .38 Smith and Wesson and examine his ID. The cop gave Bob back his badge, but kept the .38 revolver.

"You can put your hands down now."

Bob and Jill lowered their arms and relaxed.

"I bet we're after the same guys," Bob said.

"We're answering a report of gunshots."

"Hey, in here," one of the cops called from Rango's trailer.

The two policemen walked over to the Airstream with Bob and Jill. Before the cops could stop her, Jill was with them inside the trailer. She saw Pam on the bed, and then she saw the bathroom. She ran out of the trailer and collapsed in the yard, consumed by a fit of vomiting.

It was almost dawn when Gary reached Roma and the border. He parked near the international bridge and took some time to wipe the van clean of his prints. He looked at himself in the rearview and combed his hair. He would never know the truth about Pam. Maybe Rango had made her go with him, maybe not. It didn't matter any longer.

Gary opened the suitcase and counted the hundreds. There were a lot of them. He stuffed the bills into his underwear and left the keys dangling from the ignition of the van.

He walked past the U.S. customs station with the

suitcase in his hand. The border guard waved and smiled as Gary started across the Rio Grande. Gary waved back. Nobody cares when you leave a country; it's coming back that's hard.

When he got to the middle of the bridge, Gary stopped beside the mailbox that was chained to the guard rail. There was a sign on the box:

WARNING: DRUG SMUGGLING PUNISHABLE BY UP TO 15 YEARS CONFINEMENT DEPOSIT ALL DRUGS HERE

Gary looked around to make certain no one was watching, and then he opened the suitcase and dropped the bags of cocaine into the river. He shut the suitcase, and for a moment he stood on the bridge, watching the dark water flow toward the Gulf.

He looked out over the river, over the dry, rough land on both sides of the border. The pink sun rising over the desert promised a hot day. A dog barked at something on the Mexican shore. Gary knew that out there in the dawn there were Mexicans like the fellow he and Ralph had helped hurrying to make their way into Texas before it got light. They were hurrying across the river, rushing toward new lives. Sometimes all you can do is move. Gary turned and walked into the Republic of Mexico.

Dave Kuhne is Associate Director of the William L. Adams Center for Writing at Texas Christian University, where, since, 2000, he has been the editor of *descant*, TCU's literary journal. Kuhne is the author of *African Settings in Contemporary American Novels* (Greenwood Press, 1999) and principal editor of *descant: Fifty Years* (TCU Press, 2008).